GREEN TIGER'S BOOK OF CHILDREN'S POETRY

GREEN TIGER'S
BOOK OF
CHILDREN'S
POETRY

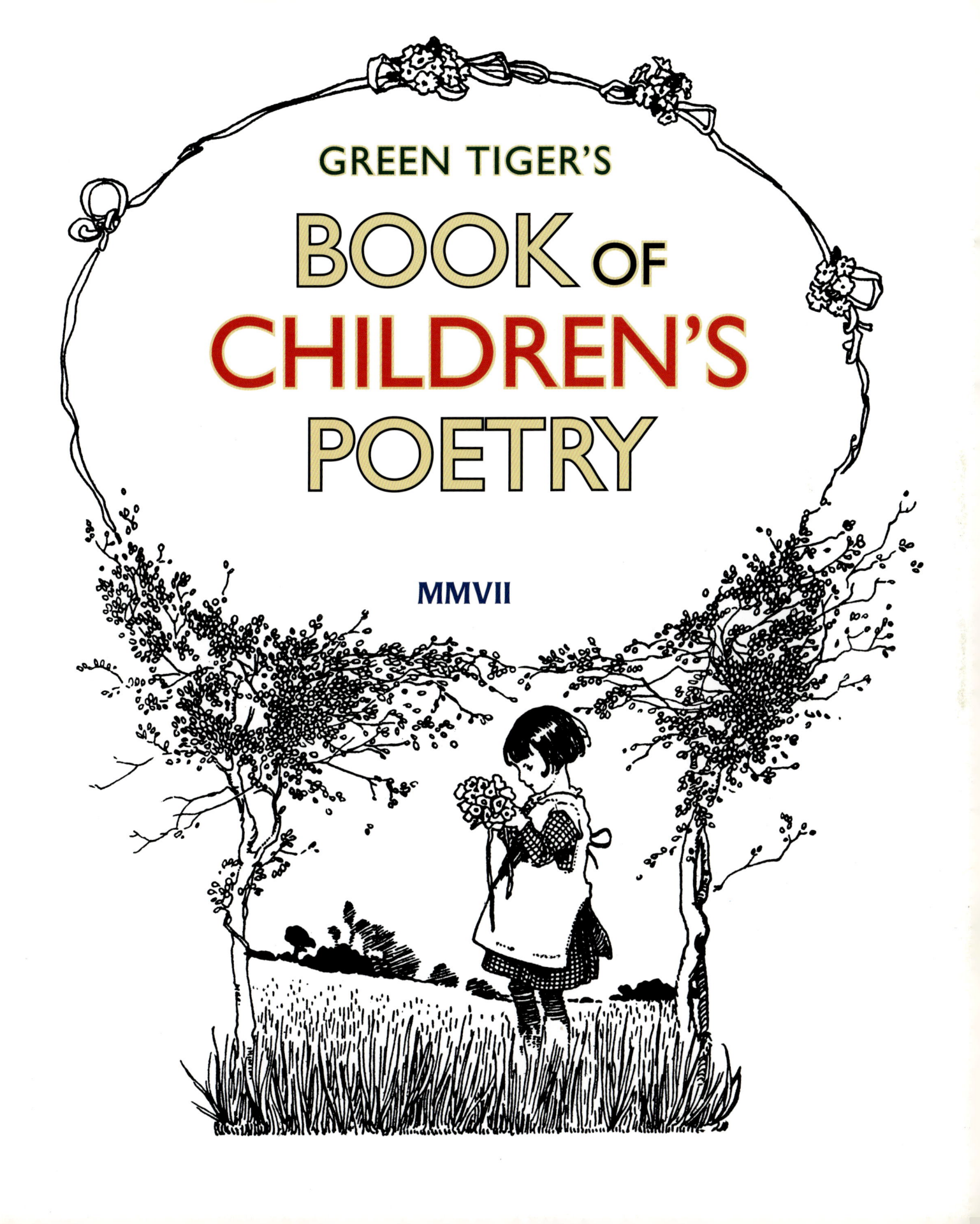

MMVII

COPYRIGHT © 2007 BLUE LANTERN STUDIO
ALL RIGHTS RESERVED   FIRST PRINTING   PRINTED IN CHINA
ISBN 978-1-59583-139-2

GREEN TIGER PRESS
A DIVISION OF LAUGHING ELEPHANT

WWW.LAUGHINGELEPHANT.COM

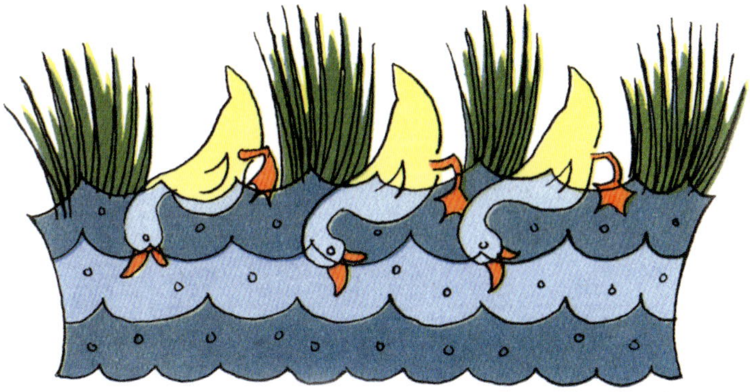

INTRODUCTION

In selecting the poems for this volume I have, of course, sought excellence, but I have also preferred variety and unfamiliarity. In reviewing numerous anthologies of children's poetry I found many of the same poems, and though these deserved their popularity, I wanted to make a little wider search in order to achieve a fresh and original gathering. There is a tendency for anthologists of children's poetry to reach a little too far into the realm of adult poetry in order to raise their readers to a higher level of appreciation. This is a very understandable and idealistic position, but it frequently leads to collections that are too difficult for young readers. I have emphasized poems that are accessible to children.

Most collections of poetry for children are gathered into sections such as "Our Animal Friends," "The Seasons," and "Play and Laughter." I have done the opposite, and have tumbled willy-nilly a bunch of poems into the volume, because I want diversity, variety and surprise. I have striven for exciting juxtapositions. I have had to resist the power of three great children's poets – Robert Louis Stevenson, Edward Lear and Eugene Field. They deserve an even greater place than they have here, but I wanted to show less familiar work, and this limited their shares in our volume.

All the poems herein are illustrated. This, of course, greatly reduced our possibilities. As with the poets we had to balance the inclusion of well known illustrators, such as Edward Lear, Jessie Willcox Smith and N.C. Wyeth, with the desire to show the work of worthwhile but largely forgotten artists. One of the things I discovered, in this search for illustrated poetry, is that humor and nonsense inspire, on the whole, better illustrations than lyric or observational verse. In making my choices I have, therefore, had to balance the value of the words and pictures. I have had to decide between fine poems with lesser illustrations, and lesser poems with excellent illustrations.

I hope the book which results from these conflicting goals pleases the child readers and their parents.

Harold Darling

2

GREEN TIGER'S BOOK OF CHILDREN'S POETRY

MY SHADOW

I have a little shadow that goes in and out with me,
And what can be the use of him is more than I can see.
He is very, very like me from the heels up to the head;
And I see him jump before me, when I jump into my bed.

The funniest thing about him is the way he likes to grow—
Not at all like proper children, which is always very slow;
For he sometimes shoots up taller like an India-rubber ball,
And he sometimes gets so little that there's none of him at all.

He hasn't got a notion of how children ought to play,
And can only make a fool of me in every sort of way.
He stays so close beside me, he's a coward you can see;
I'd think shame to stick to nursie as that shadow sticks to me.

One morning, very early, before the sun was up,
I rose and found the shining dew on every buttercup;
But my lazy little shadow, like an arrant sleepy-head,
Had stayed at home behind me and was fast asleep in bed.

Robert Louis Stevenson

GIVE ME THE SPLENDID, SILENT SUN

Give me the splendid silent sun, with all his beams full-dazzling;
Give me juicy autumnal fruit, ripe and red from the orchard;
Give me a field where the unmowed grass grows;
Give me an arbor, give me the trellised grape;
Give me fresh corn and wheat—give me serene-moving animals, teaching content;
Give me nights perfectly quiet, as on high plateaus west of the Mississippi, and I looking up at the stars;
Give me odorous at sunrise a garden of beautiful flowers, where I can walk undisturbed;
Give me for marriage a sweet-breathed woman, of whom I should never tire;
Give me a perfect child—give me, away, aside from the noise of the world, a rural, domestic life;
Give me to warble spontaneous songs, relieved, recluse by myself, for my own ears only;
Give me solitude—give me Nature—give me again, O Nature, your primal sanities!

Walt Whitman

GREEN TIGER'S BOOK OF CHILDREN'S POETRY

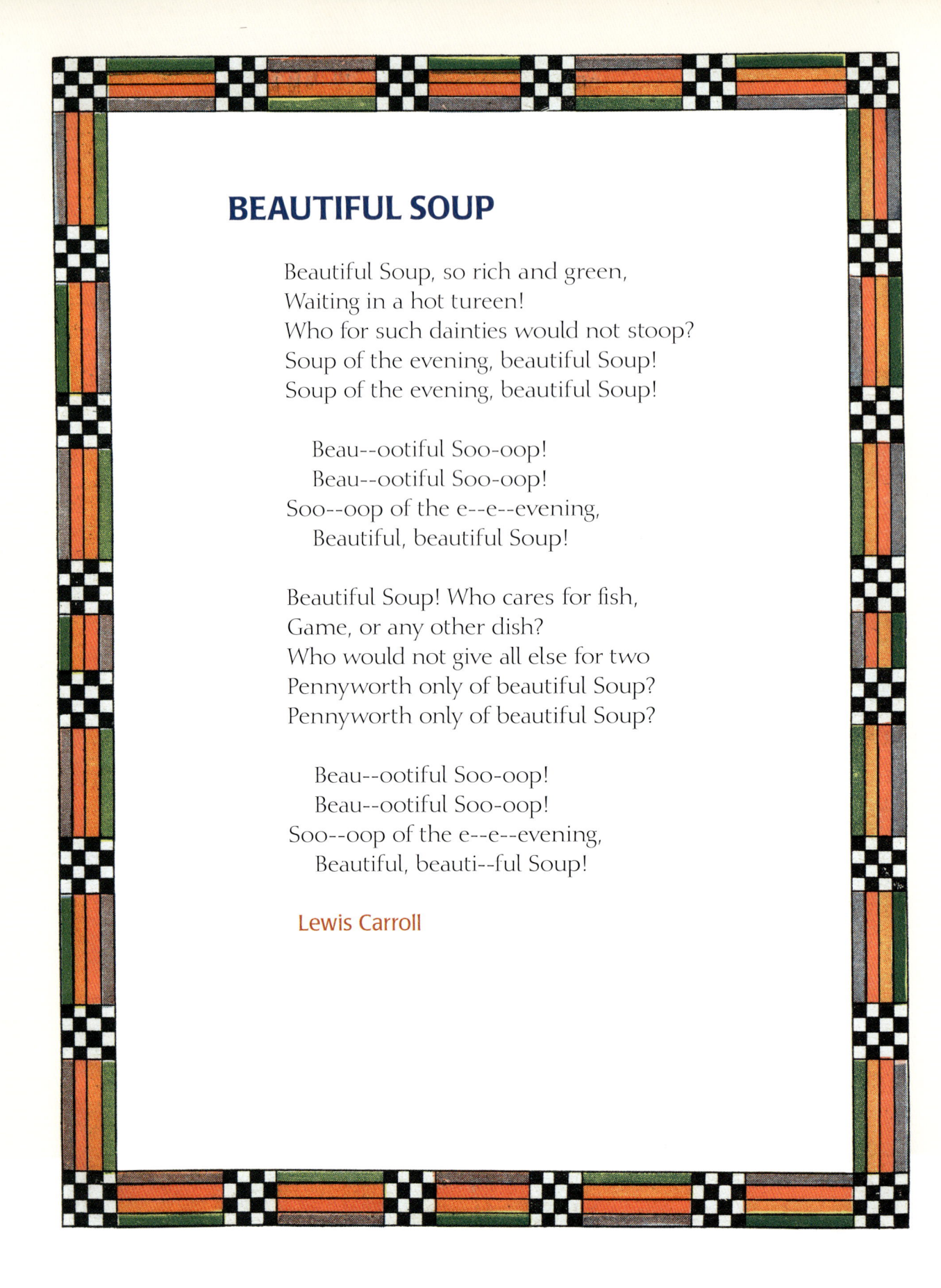

BEAUTIFUL SOUP

Beautiful Soup, so rich and green,
Waiting in a hot tureen!
Who for such dainties would not stoop?
Soup of the evening, beautiful Soup!
Soup of the evening, beautiful Soup!

    Beau--ootiful Soo-oop!
    Beau--ootiful Soo-oop!
Soo--oop of the e--e--evening,
    Beautiful, beautiful Soup!

Beautiful Soup! Who cares for fish,
Game, or any other dish?
Who would not give all else for two
Pennyworth only of beautiful Soup?
Pennyworth only of beautiful Soup?

    Beau--ootiful Soo-oop!
    Beau--ootiful Soo-oop!
Soo--oop of the e--e--evening,
    Beautiful, beauti--ful Soup!

Lewis Carroll

GREEN TIGER'S BOOK OF CHILDREN'S POETRY

HURT NO LIVING THING

Hurt no living thing:
Ladybird, nor butterfly,
Nor moth with dusty wing,
Nor cricket chirping cheerily,
Nor grasshopper so light of leap,
Nor dancing gnat, nor beetle fat,
Nor harmless worms that creep.

Christina Rossetti

GREEN TIGER'S BOOK OF CHILDREN'S POETRY

LITTLE THINGS

Little drops of water,
Little grains of sand,
Make the mighty ocean
And the pleasant land.

Thus the little minutes,
Humble though they be,
Make the mighty ages
Of eternity.

Ebenezer Cobham Brewer

Who has seen the wind?
  Neither I nor you:
But when the leaves hang trembling
  The wind is passing thro'.

Who has seen the wind?
  Neither you nor I:
But when the trees bow their heads
  The wind is passing by.

Christina Rossetti

GREEN TIGER'S BOOK OF CHILDREN'S POETRY

There was once a gorgeous Macaw.
Tried to study a work on the Law.
He'd stand by the hour
And pages devour,
While holding the book in his claw.

Walter Jerrold

Giraffes are tall,
   And their heads are high.
They stare at people
   As they go by.

Tigers are long,
   And painted with dyes.
They have soft whiskers
   And yellow eyes.

Hippos are round,
   And go at a trot.
They never gallop;
   They sleep a lot.

Camels hump up
   Where they should hump down.
Their tails are limp
   And furry and brown.

Marchette Gaylord Chute

GREEN TIGER'S BOOK OF CHILDREN'S POETRY

GIRLS AND BOYS, COME OUT TO PLAY

Girls and boys, come out to play,
   The moon is shining bright as day.
Leave your supper and leave your sleep,
   And come to your playfellows in the street.
Come with a whoop, come with a call,
   Come with a good will or not at all.
Up the ladder and down the wall,
   A halfpenny roll will serve us all.
You find milk and I'll find flour,
   And we'll have a pudding in half an hour.

Mother Goose

THE OWL AND THE PUSSYCAT

The Owl and the Pussy-cat went to sea
   In a beautiful pea green boat,
They took some honey, and plenty of money,
   Wrapped up in a five pound note.

GREEN TIGER'S BOOK OF CHILDREN'S POETRY

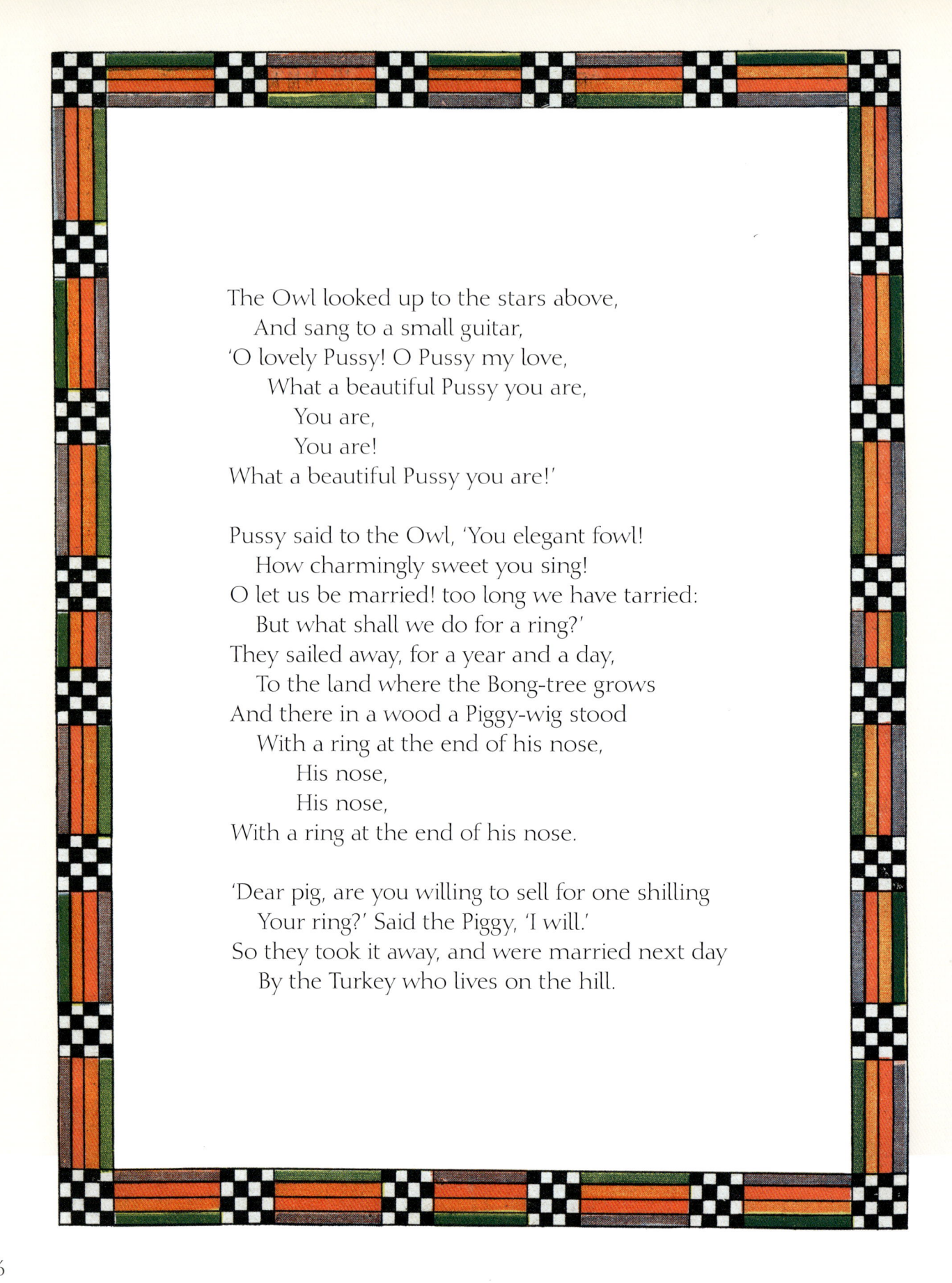

The Owl looked up to the stars above,
    And sang to a small guitar,
'O lovely Pussy! O Pussy my love,
    What a beautiful Pussy you are,
        You are,
        You are!
What a beautiful Pussy you are!'

Pussy said to the Owl, 'You elegant fowl!
    How charmingly sweet you sing!
O let us be married! too long we have tarried:
    But what shall we do for a ring?'
They sailed away, for a year and a day,
    To the land where the Bong-tree grows
And there in a wood a Piggy-wig stood
    With a ring at the end of his nose,
        His nose,
        His nose,
With a ring at the end of his nose.

'Dear pig, are you willing to sell for one shilling
    Your ring?' Said the Piggy, 'I will.'
So they took it away, and were married next day
    By the Turkey who lives on the hill.

GREEN TIGER'S BOOK OF CHILDREN'S POETRY

They dined on mince, and slices of quince,
    Which they ate with a runcible spoon;
And hand in hand, on the edge of the sand,
    They danced by the light of the moon,
        The moon,
        The moon,
They danced by the light of the moon.

Edward Lear

HAPPY THOUGHT

The world is so full of a number of Mice
I'm sure that we all should be happy and nice.

Oliver Herford

GREEN TIGER'S BOOK OF CHILDREN'S POETRY

THE SINGING CLASS

Our singing class has just begun,
There are several prizes to be won;
We've cats and kittens of every size,
And everyone hopes to win a prize.

Twice every week we meet at eight,
The study of music to cultivate;
Contralto, tenor, bass, and soprano—
Imagine the noise we make if you can O!

Our Conductor, Professor Thomas, says
That if we practice, one of these days,
He'll give a Concert and let us appear—
Then all our friends can come and hear!

C.B.

ARMIES IN THE FIRE

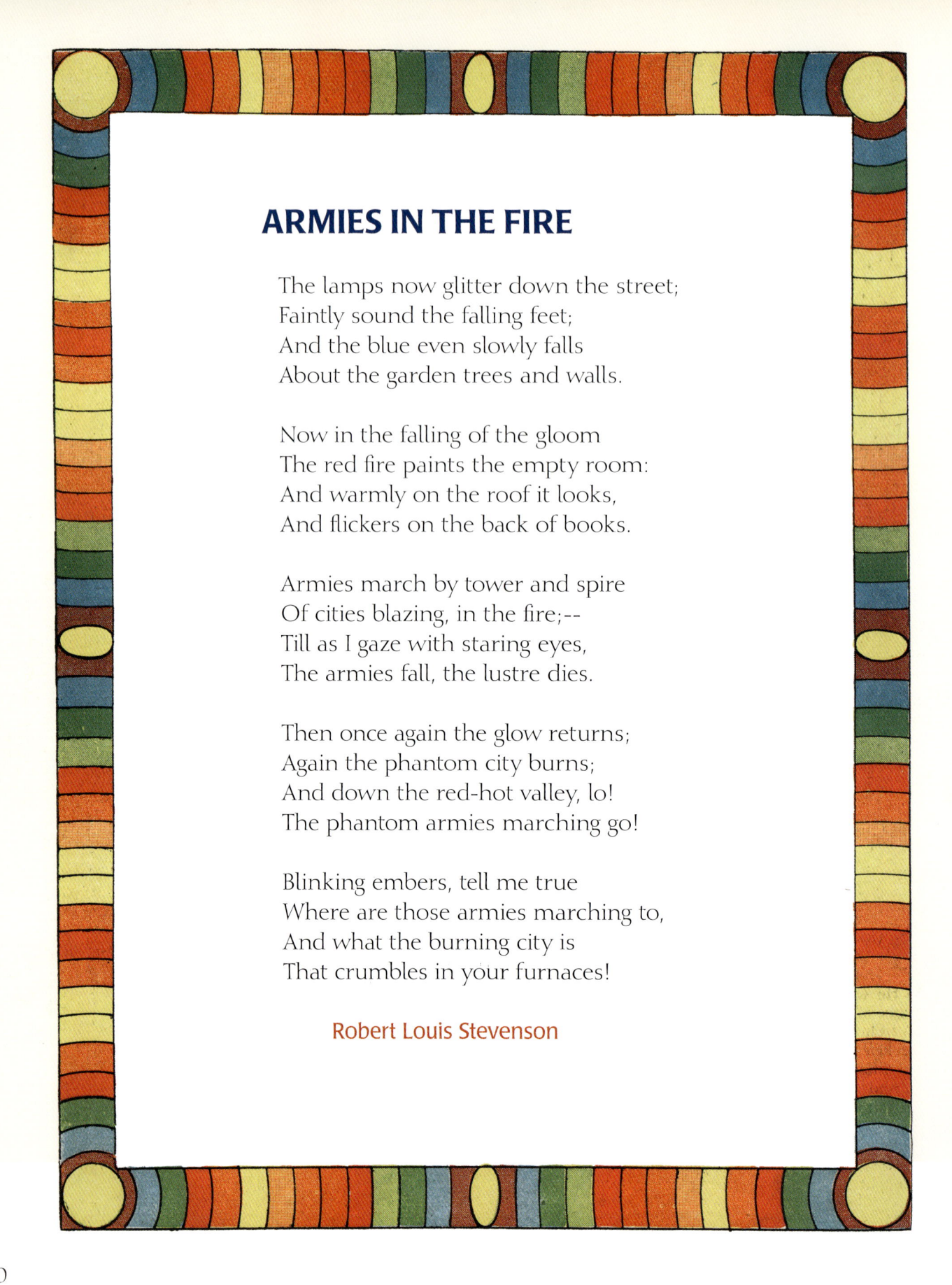

The lamps now glitter down the street;
Faintly sound the falling feet;
And the blue even slowly falls
About the garden trees and walls.

Now in the falling of the gloom
The red fire paints the empty room:
And warmly on the roof it looks,
And flickers on the back of books.

Armies march by tower and spire
Of cities blazing, in the fire;--
Till as I gaze with staring eyes,
The armies fall, the lustre dies.

Then once again the glow returns;
Again the phantom city burns;
And down the red-hot valley, lo!
The phantom armies marching go!

Blinking embers, tell me true
Where are those armies marching to,
And what the burning city is
That crumbles in your furnaces!

Robert Louis Stevenson

GREEN TIGER'S BOOK OF CHILDREN'S POETRY

THE LOAFER

A big lazy rabbit goes hopping along
Like a tramp when it's getting dark;
Or sits smoking his pipe all evening long
Like a loafer out in the park.

He hasn't a job and he hasn't got money,
And if he did have, he'd only lose 'em.
I wish children could be like this funny old bunny,
And do only the things that amuse 'em.

Monroe Stearns

GREEN TIGER'S BOOK OF CHILDREN'S POETRY

The Squirrel

Whiskey, frisky,
Hippity hop,
Up he goes
To the tree top!

Whirly, twirly,
Round and round,
Down he scampers
To the ground.

Furly, curly
What a tail!
Tall as a feather
Broad as a sail!

Where's his supper?
In the shell,
Snappity, crackity,
Out it fell.

—Unknown

THE TABLE AND THE CHAIR

Said the Table to the Chair,
"You can hardly be aware,
How I suffer from the heat,
And from chilblains on my feet!
If we took a little walk,
We might have a little talk!
Pray let us take the air!"
Said the Table to the Chair.

GREEN TIGER'S BOOK OF CHILDREN'S POETRY

II
Said the Chair to the table,
"Now you know we are not able!
How foolishly you talk,
When you know we cannot walk!"
Said the Table with a sigh,
"It can do no harm to try,
I've as many legs as you,
Why can't we walk on two?"

III
So they both went slowly down,
And walked about the town
With a cheerful bumpy sound,
As they toddled round and round.
And everybody cried,
As they hastened to their side,
"See! the Table and the Chair
Have come out to take the air!"

IV
But in going down an alley,
To a castle in a valley,
They completely lost their way,
And wandered all the day,
Till, to see them safely back,
They paid a Ducky-quack,
And a Beetle, and a Mouse,
Who took them to their house.

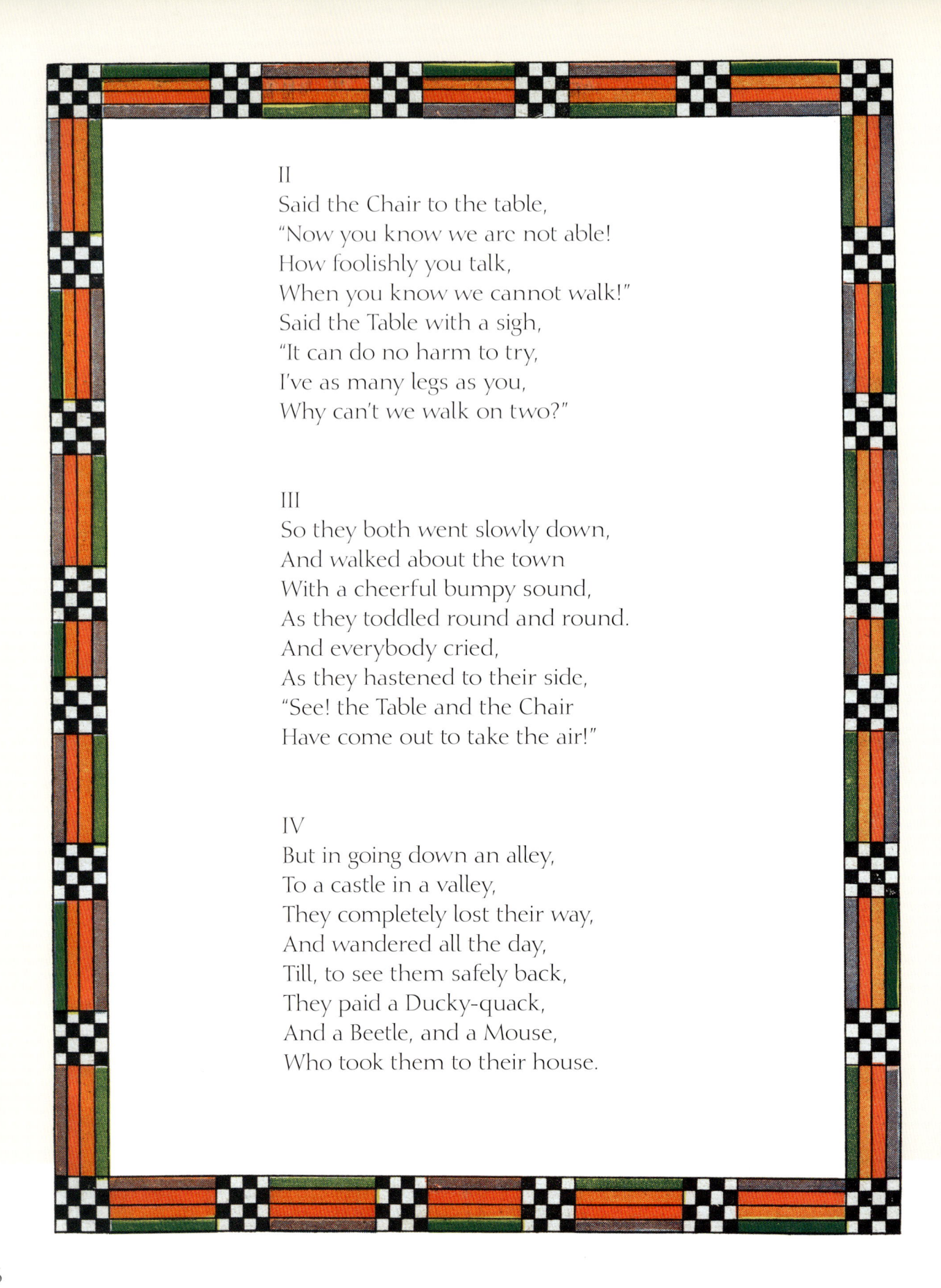

GREEN TIGER'S BOOK OF CHILDREN'S POETRY

V
Then they whispered to each other,
"O delightful little brother!
What a lovely walk we've taken!
Let us dine on Beans and Bacon!"
So the Ducky and the leetle
Browny-Mousy and the Beetle
Dined and danced upon their heads
Till they toddled to their beds.

Edward Lear

I LOVE THE FROG AND CREEPING THINGS
AND THE CRICKET THAT SO SWEETLY SINGS

I ADORE THE BEETLE AS BLACK AS INK
WHO LIVES SO SNUG BEHIND THE SINK
I DOAT ON FLIES AND MICE AND RATS

PUPPY DOGS KITTENS OR FULL GROWN CATS

I'M FOND OF A HORSE AND THE GENTLE COW

AND A TOAD THAT WOBBLES JUST ANYHOW

I LOVE THEM ALL — BOTH GREAT AND SMALL

AND WISH THAT I COULD KEEP THEM ALL

I THINK THE SNAIL A LOVELY THING

AND LIKE TO HEAR THE OSTRICH SING

BUT, I DO THINK WHERE'ER YOU GO

THERE'S NOTHING LIKE

THE FLAMINGO!

THE LAND OF COUNTERPANE

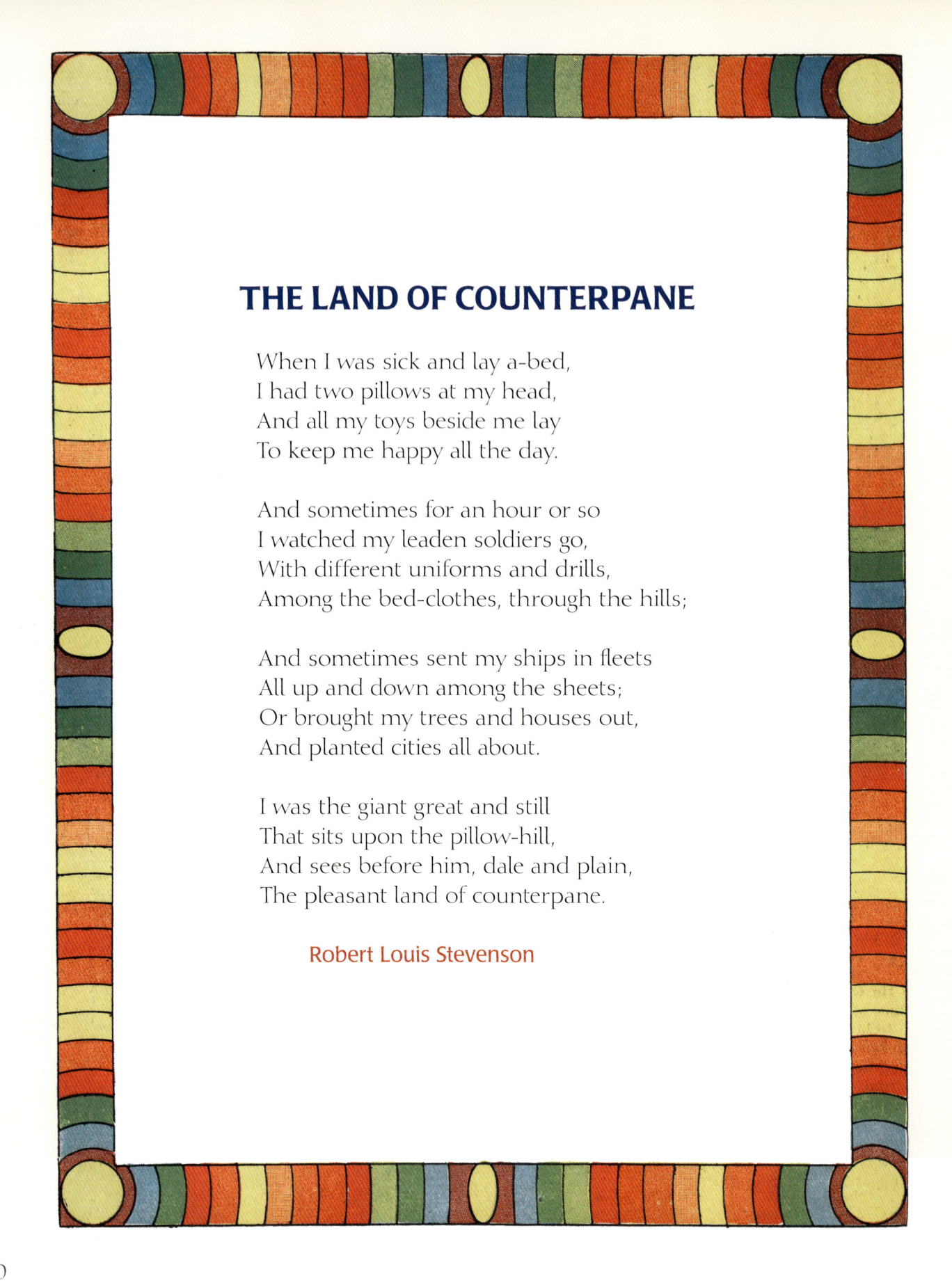

When I was sick and lay a-bed,
I had two pillows at my head,
And all my toys beside me lay
To keep me happy all the day.

And sometimes for an hour or so
I watched my leaden soldiers go,
With different uniforms and drills,
Among the bed-clothes, through the hills;

And sometimes sent my ships in fleets
All up and down among the sheets;
Or brought my trees and houses out,
And planted cities all about.

I was the giant great and still
That sits upon the pillow-hill,
And sees before him, dale and plain,
The pleasant land of counterpane.

Robert Louis Stevenson

GREEN TIGER'S BOOK OF CHILDREN'S POETRY

I WAS THE GIANT GREAT AND STILL
THAT SITS UPON THE PILLOW-HILL.

THE DUEL

The gingham dog and the calico cat
Side by side on the table sat;
'Twas half-past twelve and (what do you think!)
Nor one nor t'other had slept a wink!
The old Dutch clock and the Chinese plate
Appeared to know as sure as fate
There was going to be a terrible spat.
(I wasn't there; I simply state
What was told to me by the Chinese plate!)

The gingham dog went "bow-wow-wow!"
And the calico cat replied "mee-ow!"
The air was littered, an hour or so,
With bits of gingham and calico,
While the old Dutch clock in the chimney-place
Up with its hands before its face,
For it always dreaded a family row!
(Now mind: I'm only telling you
What the old Dutch clock declares is true!)

GREEN TIGER'S BOOK OF CHILDREN'S POETRY

The Chinese plate looked very blue,
And wailed, "Oh, dear! What shall we do!"
But the gingham dog and the calico cat
Wallowed this way and tumbled that,
Employing every tooth and claw
In the awfullest way you ever saw–
And, oh! How the gingham and calico flew!
(Don't fancy I exaggerate–
I got my news from the Chinese plate!)

Next morning, where the two had sat
They found no trace of dog or cat;
And some folks think unto this day
That burglars stole that pair away!
But the truth about the cat and pup
Is this: They ate each other up!
Now what do you really think of that!
(The old Dutch clock it told me so,
And that is how I came to know.)

Eugene Field

GREEN TIGER'S BOOK OF CHILDREN'S POETRY

OLD MOTHER ROCKER

Old Mother Rocker
Will hold you in her lap
When you are tired and weary
And want to have a nap.

Willard Bonte

RECKLESS ROBIN

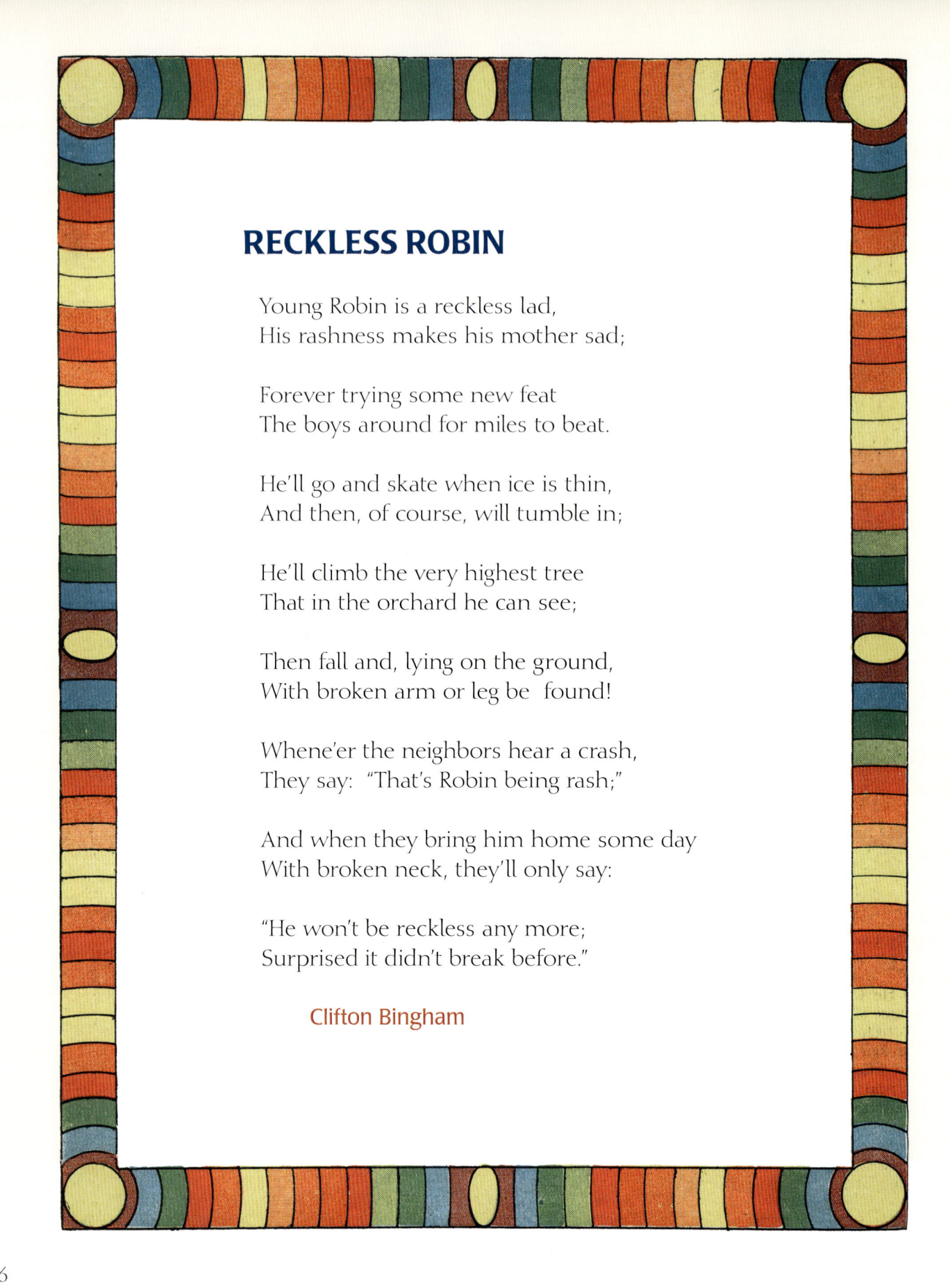

Young Robin is a reckless lad,
His rashness makes his mother sad;

Forever trying some new feat
The boys around for miles to beat.

He'll go and skate when ice is thin,
And then, of course, will tumble in;

He'll climb the very highest tree
That in the orchard he can see;

Then fall and, lying on the ground,
With broken arm or leg be found!

Whene'er the neighbors hear a crash,
They say: "That's Robin being rash;"

And when they bring him home some day
With broken neck, they'll only say:

"He won't be reckless any more;
Surprised it didn't break before."

    Clifton Bingham

GREEN TIGER'S BOOK OF CHILDREN'S POETRY

A VERY HAPPY FAMILY

The Mother sings a song of Youth and May,
The Father doth the festive fiddle play,
Neighbors strolling on the fence
Stop and smile with joy intense,
While the happy kittens dance the livelong day.

J.G. Francis

ANIMAL CRACKERS

Animal crackers and cocoa to drink,
That is the finest of suppers I think;
When I'm grown up and can have what I please
I think I shall always insist upon these.

What do YOU choose when you're offered a treat?
When Mother says, "What would you like best to eat?"
Is it waffles and syrup, or cinnamon toast?
It's cocoa and animals that I love the most!

The kitchen's the coziest place that I know;
The kettle is singing, the stove is aglow,
And there in the twilight, how jolly to see
The cocoa and animals waiting for me.

Daddy and Mother dine later in state,
With Mary to cook for them, Susan to wait;
But they don't have nearly as much fun as I
Who eat in the kitchen with Nurse standing by;
And Daddy once said, he would like to be me
Having cocoa and animals once more for tea!

           Christopher Morley

There was an Old Man of Peru,
Who never knew what he should do;
So he tore off his hair,
And behaved like a bear,
That intrinsic Old Man of Peru.

There was an Old Man of the West,
Who never could get any rest;
So they set him to spin
On his nose and his chin,
Which cured that Old Man of the West.

GREEN TIGER'S BOOK OF CHILDREN'S POETRY

There was an Old Man who supposed,
That the street door was partially closed;
But some very large rats,
Ate his coats and his hats,
While that futile Old Gentleman dozed.

Edward Lear

GREAT, WIDE, BEAUTIFUL, WONDERFUL WORLD

Great, wide, beautiful, wonderful World,
With the wonderful water round you curled,
And the wonderful grass upon your breast--
World, you are beautifully drest.

The wonderful air is over me,
And the wonderful wind is shaking the tree,
It walks on the water, and whirls the mills,
And talks to itself on the tops of the hills.

You friendly Earth! how far do you go,
With the wheat-fields that nod and the rivers that flow,
With cities and gardens, and cliffs and isles,
And people upon you for thousands of miles?

Ah, you are so great, and I am so small,
I tremble to think of you, World, at all;
And yet, when I said my prayers to-day,
A whisper inside me seemed to say,
"You are more than the Earth, though you are such a
dot: You can love and think, and the Earth cannot!"

William Brighty Rands

GREEN TIGER'S BOOK OF CHILDREN'S POETRY

THE LOLLIPOPINJAY

On lollipops I live. I'm gay;
I leap and swirl, I spin and sway.
Come join me in the dance, I pray!
Let's go!—Slap-bang!—Hip, hip, hooray!

For I'm the lollipopinjay.
I loll by night, I dance all day.
I jump, I crouch and pop away
Skip! Hop!– Tip-top!– Hip, hip, hooray!

Hugh Lofting

SAND

A funny kind of ground is sand,
It's not exactly muddy,
And it's not exactly land.
And you can build for hours
To make castles grand and tall,
But when you come again next day
You can't find them at all.

Phyllis Britcher

PICTURE-BOOKS IN WINTER

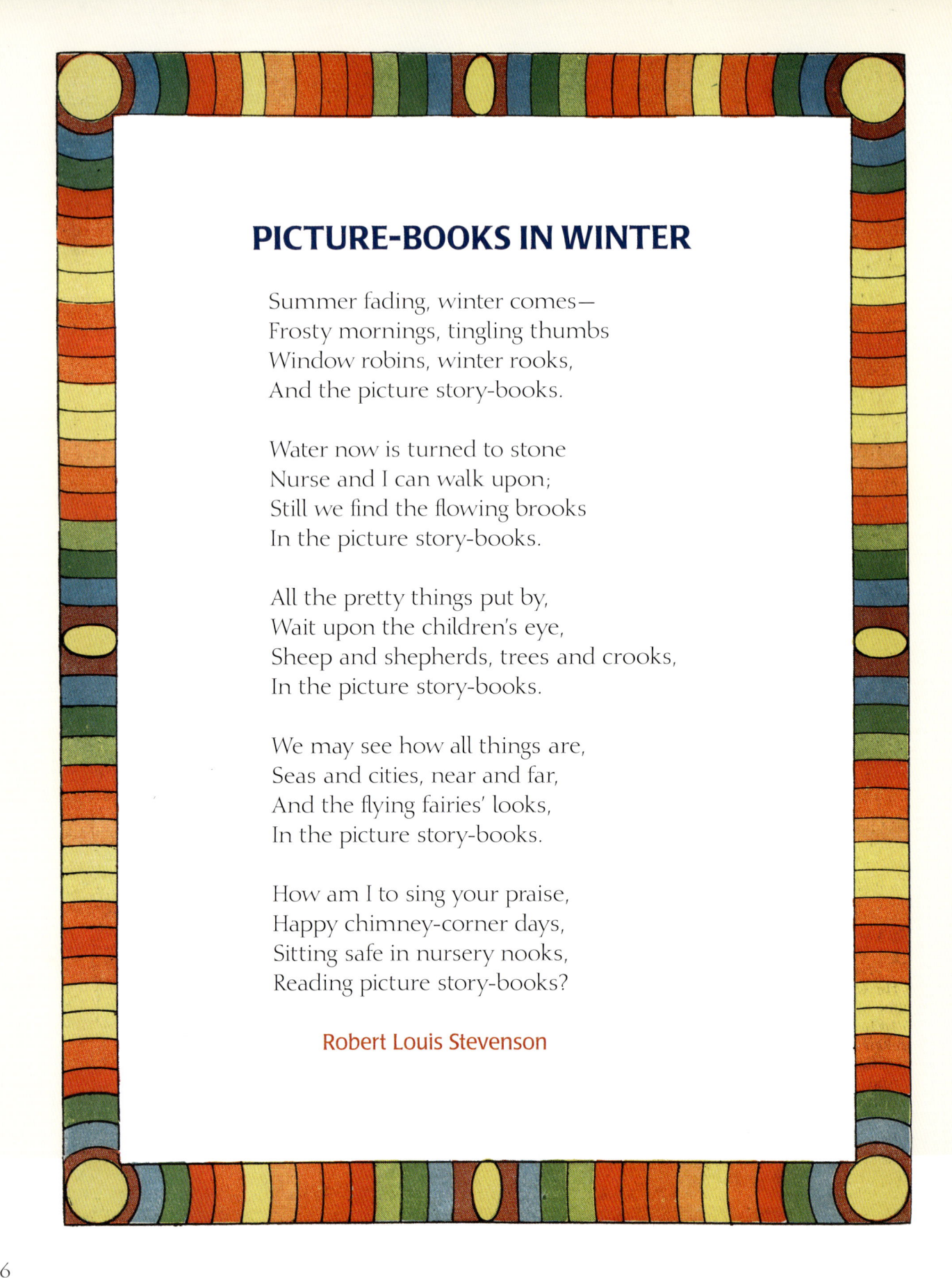

Summer fading, winter comes—
Frosty mornings, tingling thumbs
Window robins, winter rooks,
And the picture story-books.

Water now is turned to stone
Nurse and I can walk upon;
Still we find the flowing brooks
In the picture story-books.

All the pretty things put by,
Wait upon the children's eye,
Sheep and shepherds, trees and crooks,
In the picture story-books.

We may see how all things are,
Seas and cities, near and far,
And the flying fairies' looks,
In the picture story-books.

How am I to sing your praise,
Happy chimney-corner days,
Sitting safe in nursery nooks,
Reading picture story-books?

Robert Louis Stevenson

GREEN TIGER'S BOOK OF CHILDREN'S POETRY

FRIEND FOREST-HORSE

Friend Forest-horse is bold,
Sagacious, and serene,
Walking through the rainbow,
And the gold,
And taking in the scene.

Vachel Lindsay

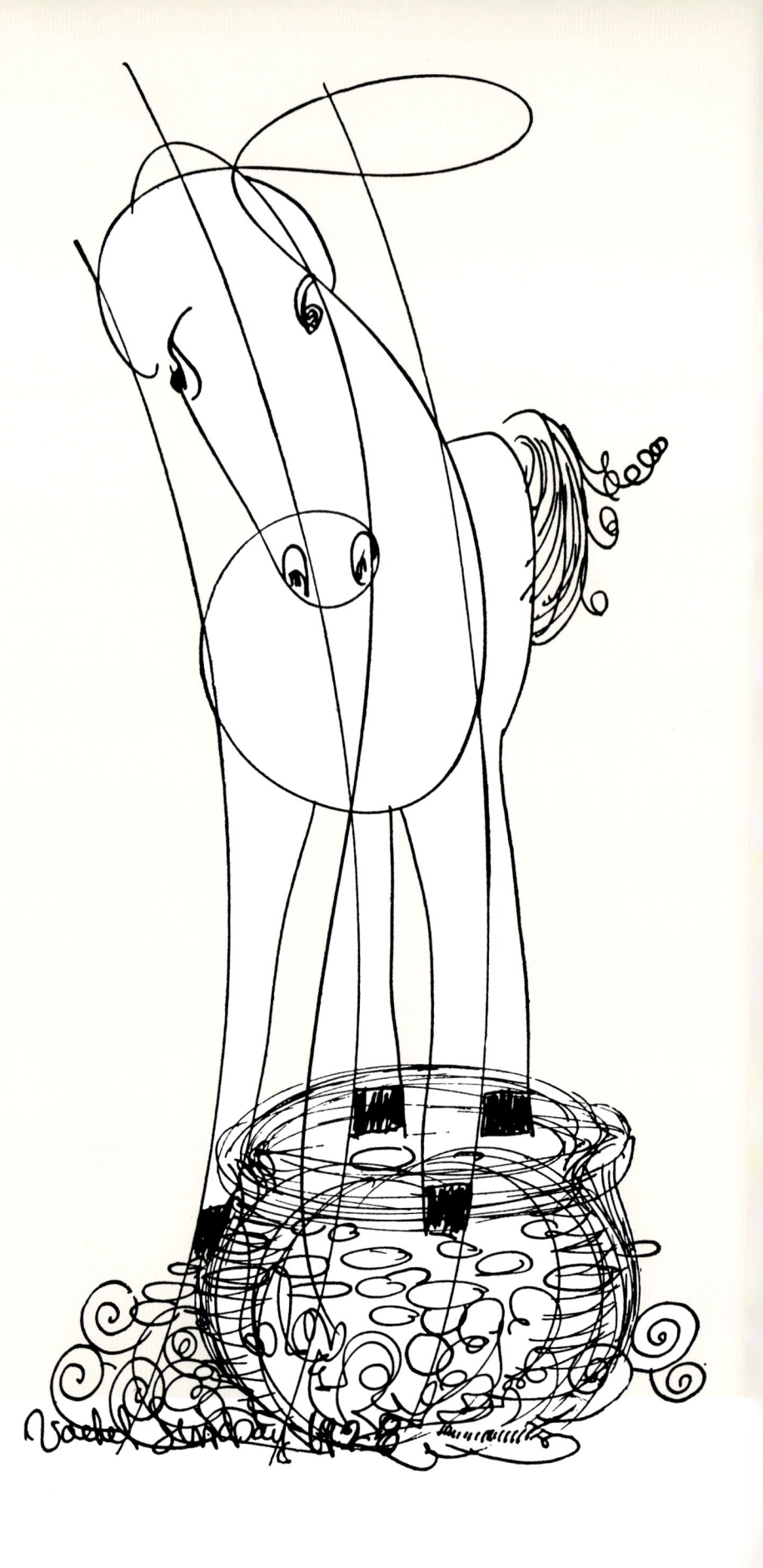

GREEN TIGER'S BOOK OF CHILDREN'S POETRY

BRINGING UP KITTENS

"There's lots of things you must not forget,"
The mother cat tells her daughter.
"Be careful of getting your little paws wet,
And never fall into the water.

Don't waste your time hunting birds in flight;
Be careful of bones in fish.
When you meet strange dogs, keep a tree in sight;
And don't let them near your dish."

Monroe Stearns

ESCAPE AT BEDTIME

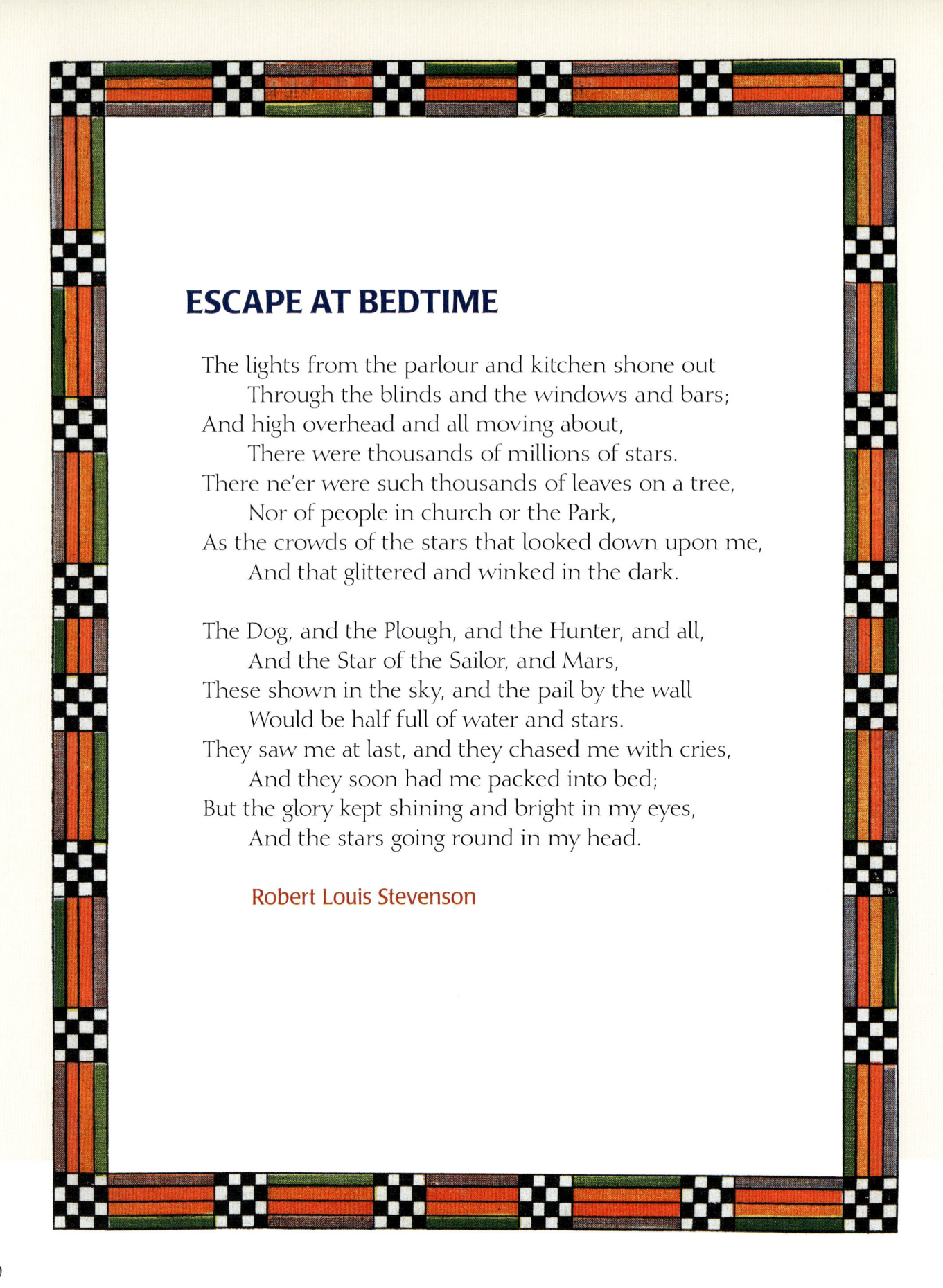

The lights from the parlour and kitchen shone out
    Through the blinds and the windows and bars;
And high overhead and all moving about,
    There were thousands of millions of stars.
There ne'er were such thousands of leaves on a tree,
    Nor of people in church or the Park,
As the crowds of the stars that looked down upon me,
    And that glittered and winked in the dark.

The Dog, and the Plough, and the Hunter, and all,
    And the Star of the Sailor, and Mars,
These shown in the sky, and the pail by the wall
    Would be half full of water and stars.
They saw me at last, and they chased me with cries,
    And they soon had me packed into bed;
But the glory kept shining and bright in my eyes,
    And the stars going round in my head.

Robert Louis Stevenson

GREEN TIGER'S BOOK OF CHILDREN'S POETRY

ELETELEPHONY

Once there was an elephant,
Who tried to use the telephant—

No! No! I mean an elephone
Who tried to use the telephone—

(Dear me! I am not certain quite
That even now I've got it right.)

Howe'er it was, he got his trunk
Entangled in the telephunk;

The more he tried to get it free,
The louder buzzed the telephee—

(I fear I'd better drop the song
Of elephop and telephong!)

Laura Elizabeth Richards

GARDEN FAIRIES

Fairies in the garden, O!
In the garden tippy-toe,
Here they come! Here they go!

In the grass and in the air,
You can't catch them anywhere!
Fairies playing tag-your-wing,
Hear them sing! Hear them sing!

Fairies sliding down the hills,
Hiding in the daffodils,
Hiding from all grown-up eyes
On their airplane butterflies.

Here they come! Here they go!
In the garden tippy-toe,
Fairies in the garden, O!

Marjorie Barrows

GREEN TIGER'S BOOK OF CHILDREN'S POETRY

OUR VISIT TO THE ZOO

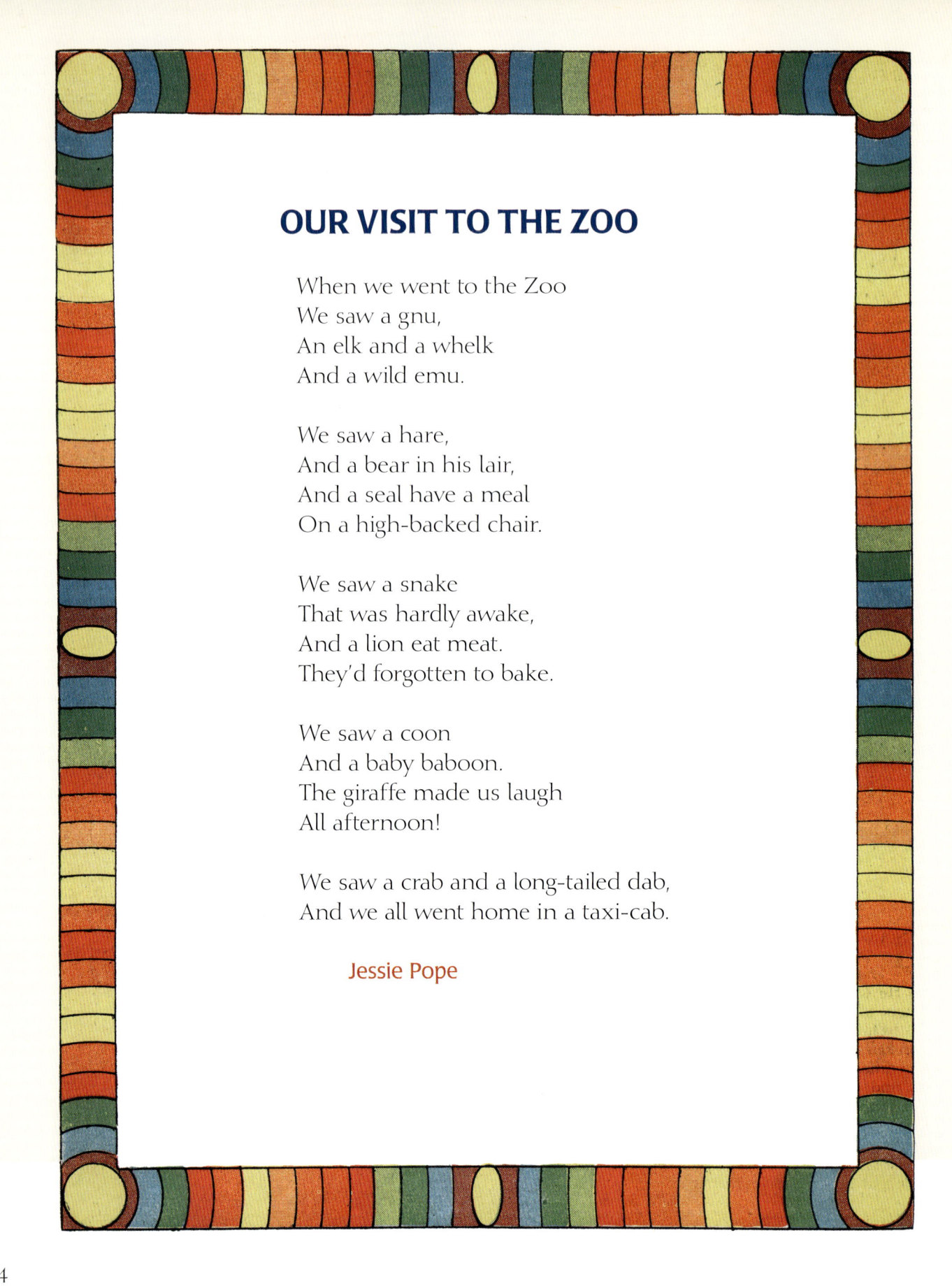

When we went to the Zoo
We saw a gnu,
An elk and a whelk
And a wild emu.

We saw a hare,
And a bear in his lair,
And a seal have a meal
On a high-backed chair.

We saw a snake
That was hardly awake,
And a lion eat meat.
They'd forgotten to bake.

We saw a coon
And a baby baboon.
The giraffe made us laugh
All afternoon!

We saw a crab and a long-tailed dab,
And we all went home in a taxi-cab.

Jessie Pope

GREEN TIGER'S BOOK OF CHILDREN'S POETRY

THE SUNSET GARDEN

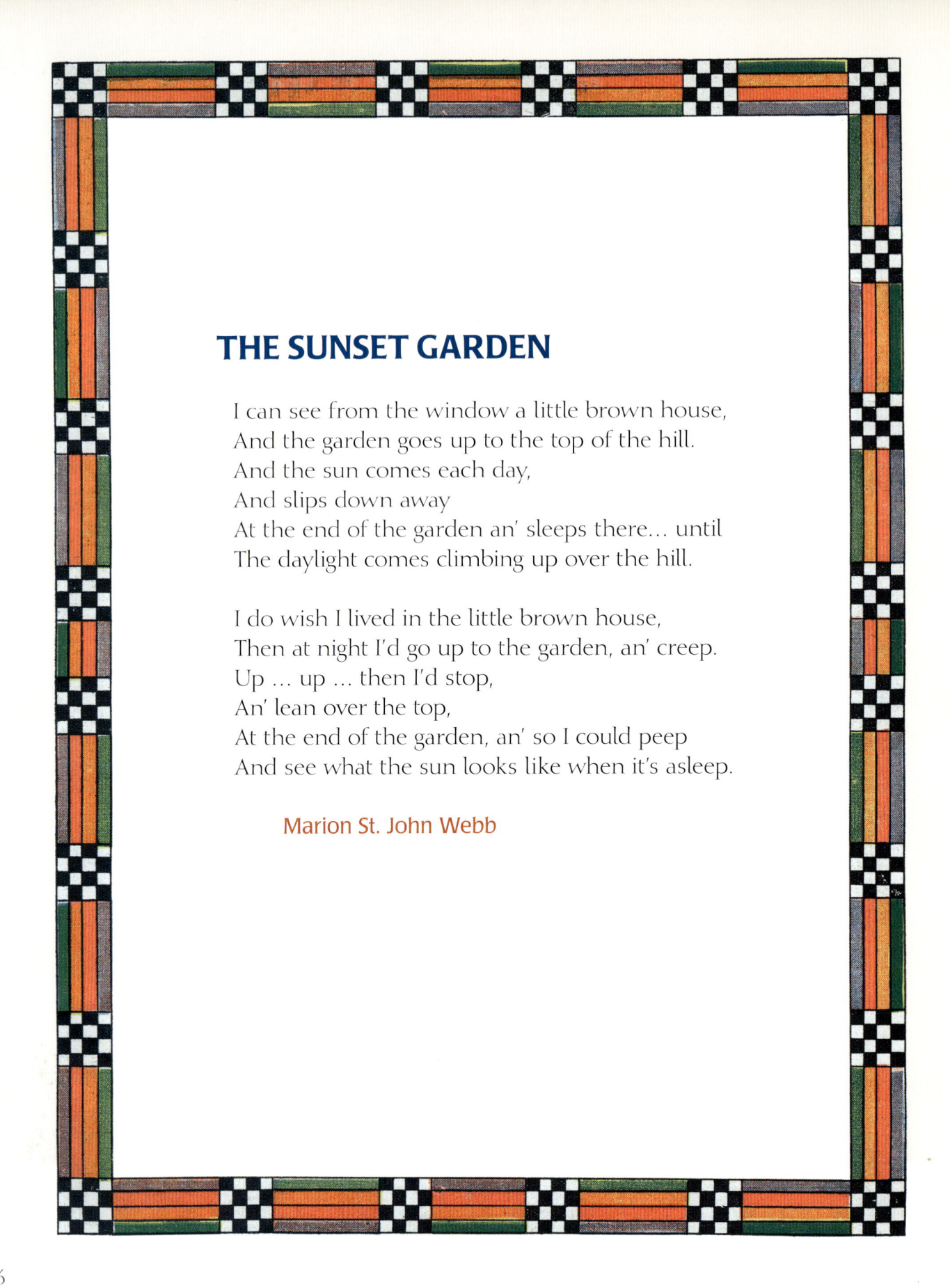

I can see from the window a little brown house,
And the garden goes up to the top of the hill.
And the sun comes each day,
And slips down away
At the end of the garden an' sleeps there… until
The daylight comes climbing up over the hill.

I do wish I lived in the little brown house,
Then at night I'd go up to the garden, an' creep.
Up … up … then I'd stop,
An' lean over the top,
At the end of the garden, an' so I could peep
And see what the sun looks like when it's asleep.

Marion St. John Webb

GREEN TIGER'S BOOK OF CHILDREN'S POETRY

THE ELEPHANT

When people call this beast to mind,
 They marvel more and more
At such a little tail behind,
 So LARGE a trunk before.

Hilaire Belloc

GREEN TIGER'S BOOK OF CHILDREN'S POETRY

THE PURPLE COW

I never saw a Purple Cow
I never hope to *see* one
But I can tell you anyhow
I'd rather *see* than *be* one.

Gelett Burgess

SWEET AND LOW

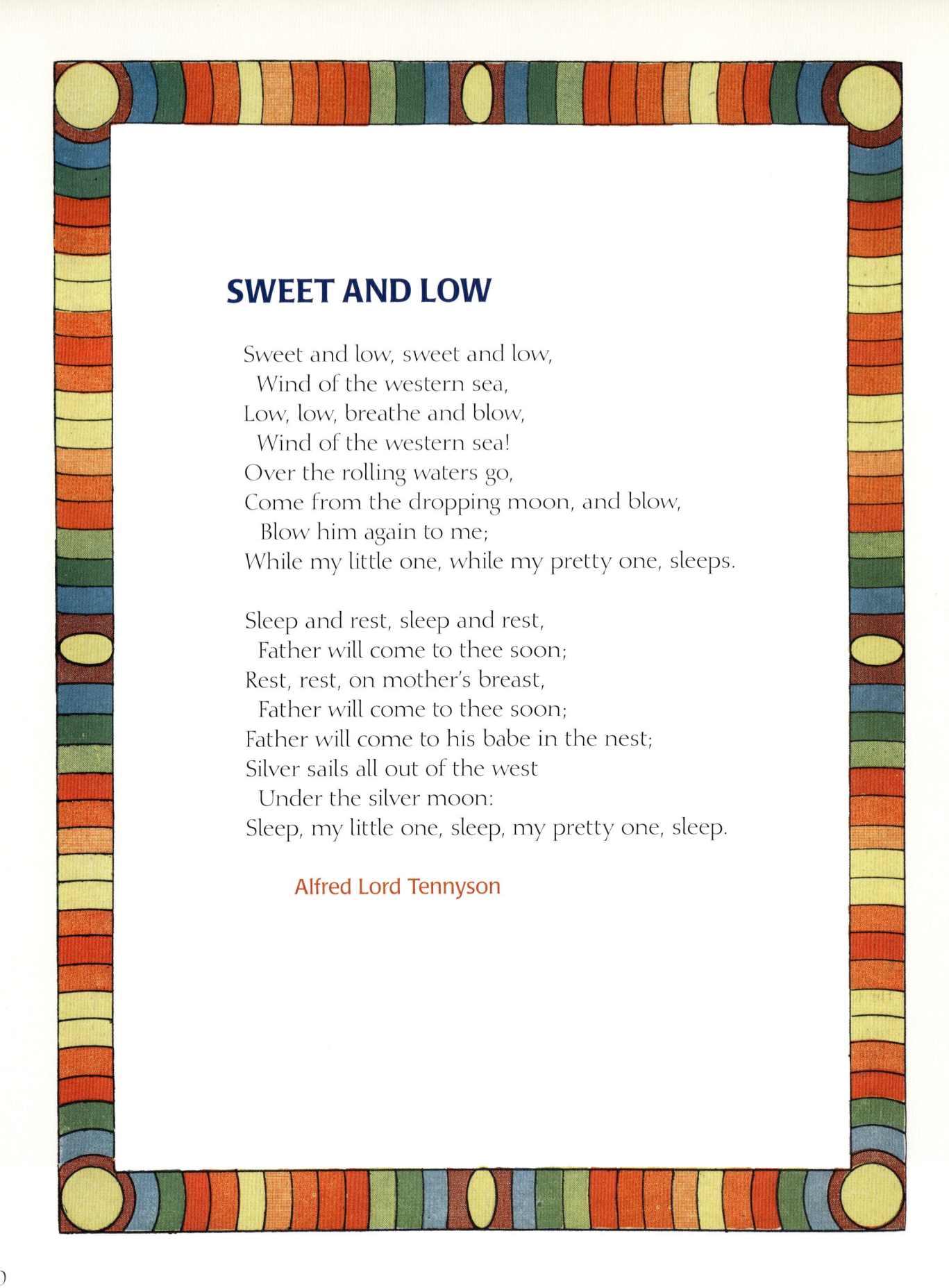

Sweet and low, sweet and low,
  Wind of the western sea,
Low, low, breathe and blow,
  Wind of the western sea!
Over the rolling waters go,
Come from the dropping moon, and blow,
  Blow him again to me;
While my little one, while my pretty one, sleeps.

Sleep and rest, sleep and rest,
  Father will come to thee soon;
Rest, rest, on mother's breast,
  Father will come to thee soon;
Father will come to his babe in the nest;
Silver sails all out of the west
  Under the silver moon:
Sleep, my little one, sleep, my pretty one, sleep.

Alfred Lord Tennyson

GREEN TIGER'S BOOK OF CHILDREN'S POETRY

THE BAD POTATO

This young potato oft was told,
By people who were wise and old,
That it is very far from right
To read without sufficient light.
He heeded not their wise behest,
But when the sun sank in the west,
He strained his eyes by twilight dim,
And goggles soon were put on him.
Dearie, will you this lesson heed?
And after sundown do not read.

Carolyn Wells

PENSIVE PERCY

Percy when a little boy
Was quiet as a mouse,
He never set the barn afire
Nor battered down the house.

He used to sit for hours and hours
Just gazing at the moon,
And feeding little fishes
Sarsaparilla from a spoon.

Leroy F. Jackson

WYNKEN, BLYNKEN, AND NOD

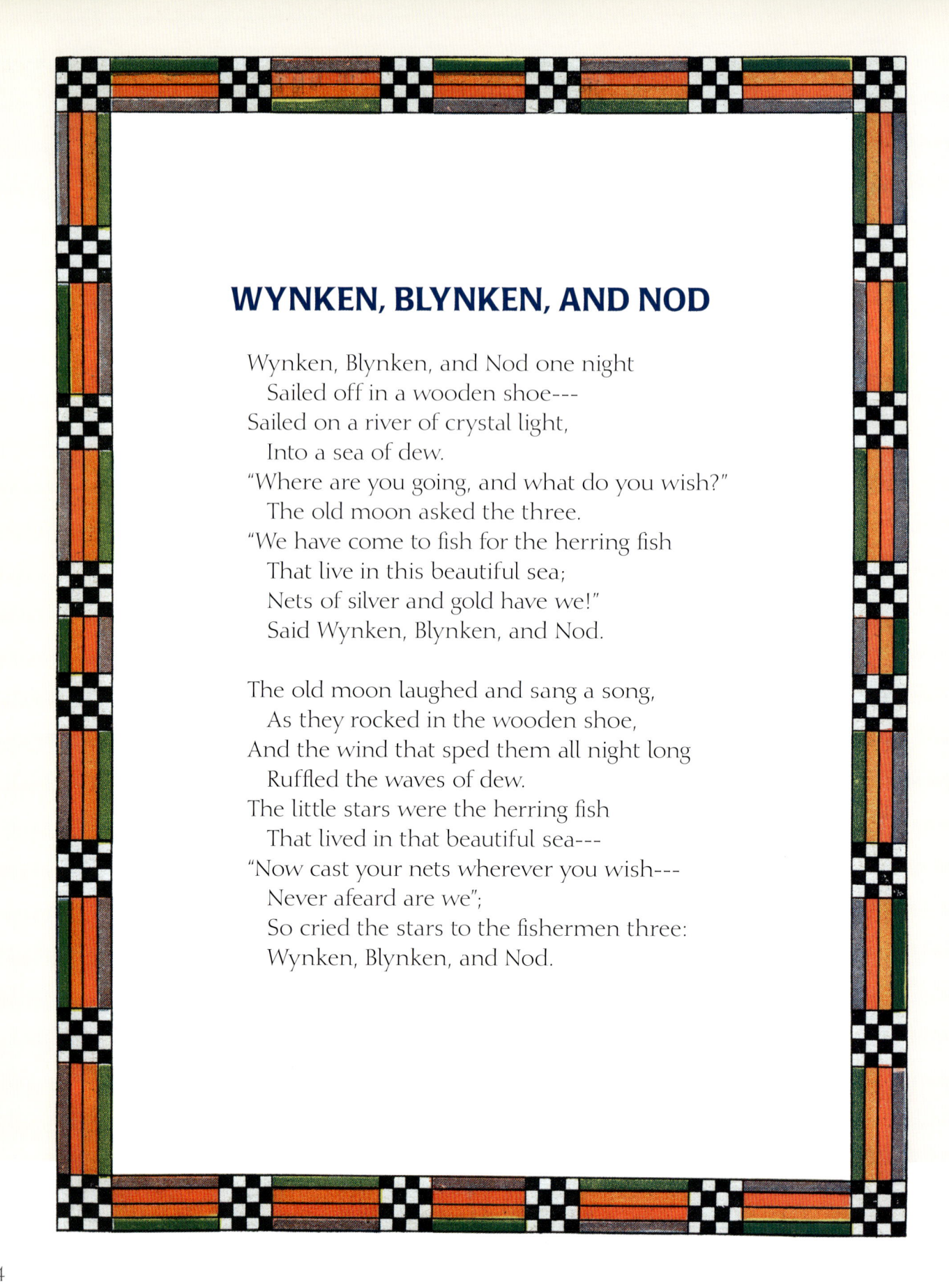

Wynken, Blynken, and Nod one night
   Sailed off in a wooden shoe---
Sailed on a river of crystal light,
   Into a sea of dew.
"Where are you going, and what do you wish?"
   The old moon asked the three.
"We have come to fish for the herring fish
   That live in this beautiful sea;
   Nets of silver and gold have we!"
   Said Wynken, Blynken, and Nod.

The old moon laughed and sang a song,
   As they rocked in the wooden shoe,
And the wind that sped them all night long
   Ruffled the waves of dew.
The little stars were the herring fish
   That lived in that beautiful sea---
"Now cast your nets wherever you wish---
   Never afeard are we";
   So cried the stars to the fishermen three:
   Wynken, Blynken, and Nod.

GREEN TIGER'S BOOK OF CHILDREN'S POETRY

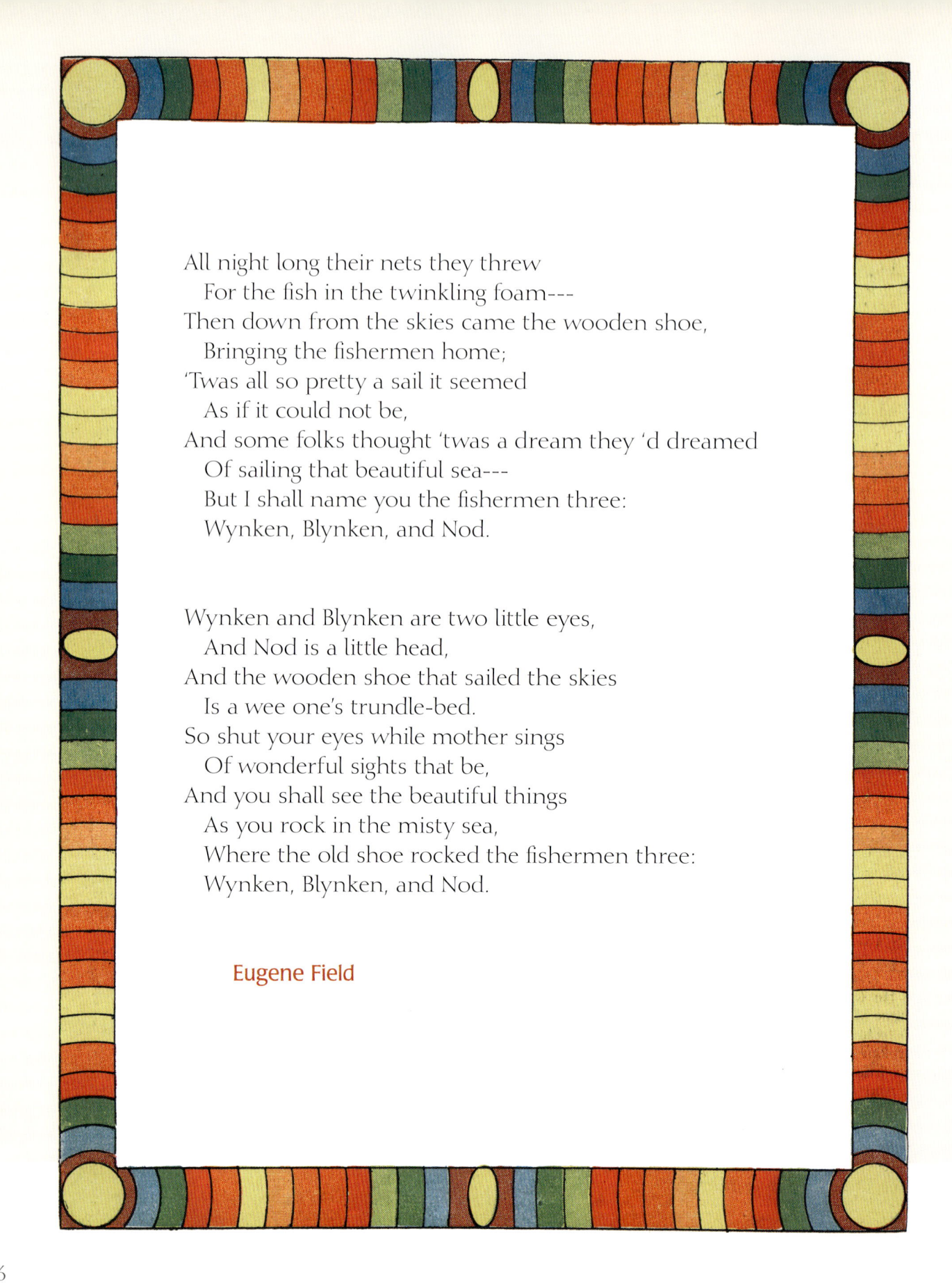

All night long their nets they threw
   For the fish in the twinkling foam---
Then down from the skies came the wooden shoe,
   Bringing the fishermen home;
'Twas all so pretty a sail it seemed
   As if it could not be,
And some folks thought 'twas a dream they 'd dreamed
   Of sailing that beautiful sea---
   But I shall name you the fishermen three:
   Wynken, Blynken, and Nod.

Wynken and Blynken are two little eyes,
   And Nod is a little head,
And the wooden shoe that sailed the skies
   Is a wee one's trundle-bed.
So shut your eyes while mother sings
   Of wonderful sights that be,
And you shall see the beautiful things
   As you rock in the misty sea,
   Where the old shoe rocked the fishermen three:
   Wynken, Blynken, and Nod.

Eugene Field

GREEN TIGER'S BOOK OF CHILDREN'S POETRY

THE BEAUTIFUL SWAN

All day she rules the pond from edge to edge,
Exerting Beauty's easy privileges;
Her world a mirror spread in each direction,
Where she reflects upon her own reflection.

Arthur Waugh

LET'S PRETEND

Let's pretend we're elephants
Who trample down tall grass
Who force their way through jungles
And trumpet as they pass.

James S. Tippett.

GREEN TIGER'S BOOK OF CHILDREN'S POETRY

Bonny lass, bonny lass,
Wilt thou be mine?
Thou shalt not wash dishes,
Nor yet feed the swine.

But sit on a cushion,
And sew a fine seam,
And thou shalt eat strawberries,
Sugar, and cream.

Unknown

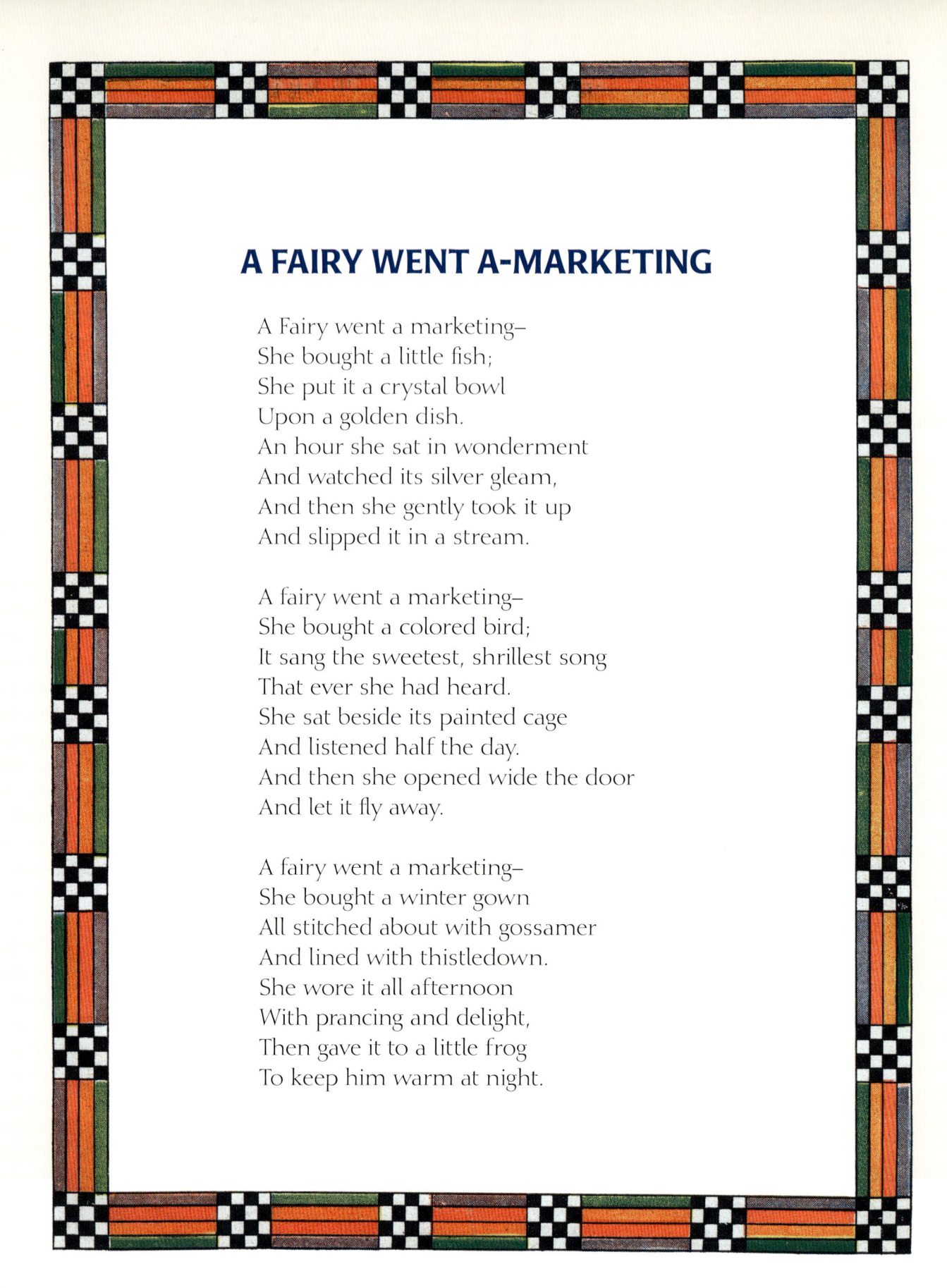

A FAIRY WENT A-MARKETING

A Fairy went a marketing–
She bought a little fish;
She put it a crystal bowl
Upon a golden dish.
An hour she sat in wonderment
And watched its silver gleam,
And then she gently took it up
And slipped it in a stream.

A fairy went a marketing–
She bought a colored bird;
It sang the sweetest, shrillest song
That ever she had heard.
She sat beside its painted cage
And listened half the day.
And then she opened wide the door
And let it fly away.

A fairy went a marketing–
She bought a winter gown
All stitched about with gossamer
And lined with thistledown.
She wore it all afternoon
With prancing and delight,
Then gave it to a little frog
To keep him warm at night.

GREEN TIGER'S BOOK OF CHILDREN'S POETRY

A fairy went a-marketing–
She bought a gentle mouse
To take her tiny messages,
To keep her tiny house.
All day she kept its busy feet
Pit-patting to and fro,
And then she kissed its silken ears,
Thanked it, and let it go.

   Rose Fyleman

SOLUTION

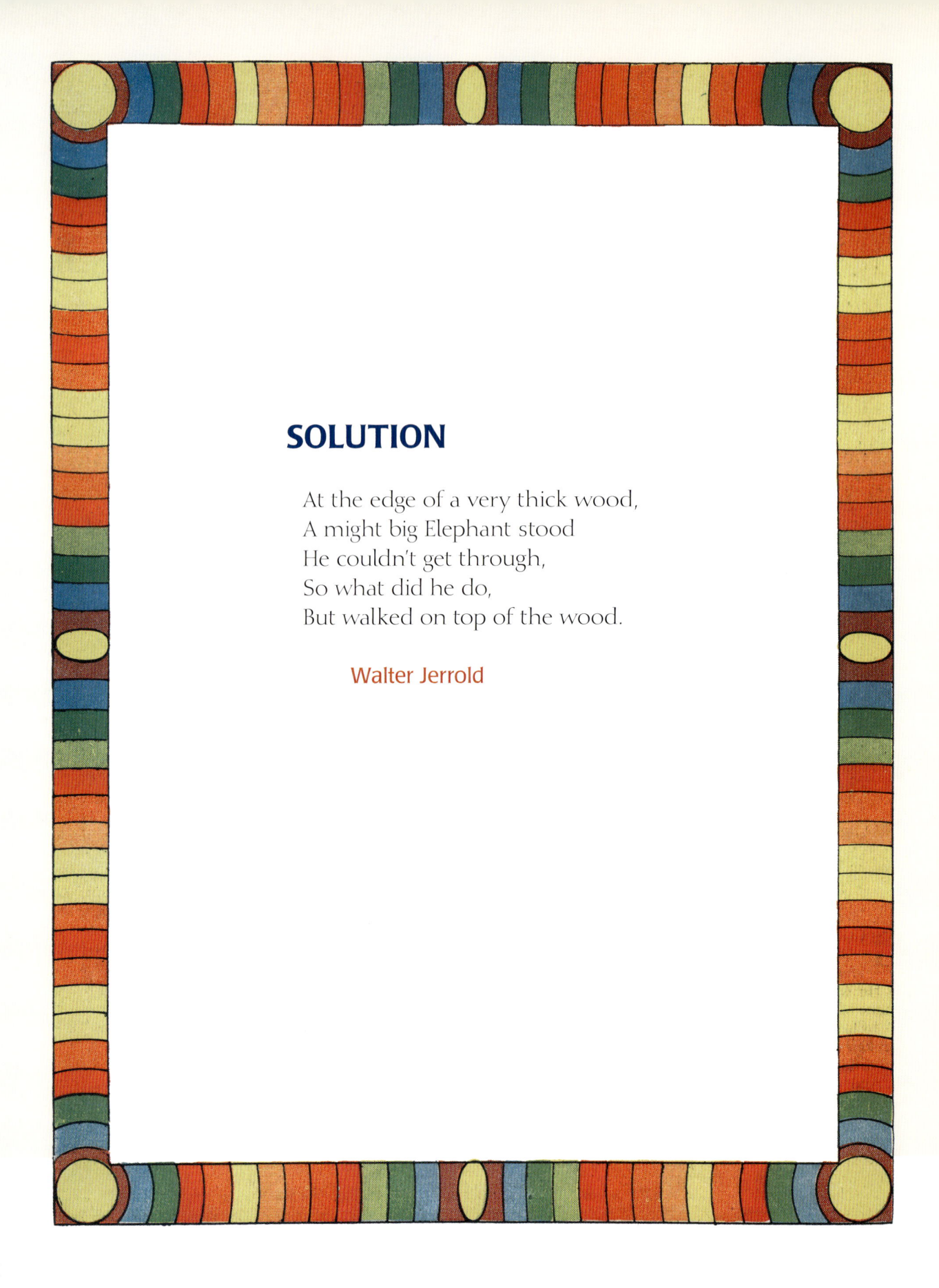

At the edge of a very thick wood,
A might big Elephant stood
He couldn't get through,
So what did he do,
But walked on top of the wood.

Walter Jerrold

GREEN TIGER'S BOOK OF CHILDREN'S POETRY

APRIL RAIN SONG

Let the rain kiss you.
Let the rain beat upon your head with silver liquid drops.
Let the rain sing you a lullaby.
The rain makes still pools on the sidewalk.
The rain makes running pools in the gutter.
The rain plays a little sleep song on our roof at night.
And I love the rain.

Langston Hughes

GREEN TIGER'S BOOK OF CHILDREN'S POETRY

TIME TO RISE

A birdie with a yellow bill
Hopped upon the window sill,
Cocked his shining eye and said:
"Ain't you 'shamed, you sleepy-head?"

Robert Louis Stevenson

ANSWER TO A CHILD'S QUESTION

Do you ask what the birds say? The Sparrow, the Dove,
The Linnet and Thrush say, "I love and I love!"
In the winter they're silent -- the wind is so strong;
What it says, I don't know, but it sings a loud song.
But green leaves, and blossoms, and sunny warm weather,
And singing, and loving -- all come back together.
But the Lark is so brimful of gladness and love,
The green fields below him, the blue sky above,
That he sings, and he sings; and forever sings he --
I love my Love, and my Love loves me!

Samuel Taylor Coleridge

GREEN TIGER'S BOOK OF CHILDREN'S POETRY

CALICO PIE

    Calico Pie,
      The little Birds fly
Down to the calico tree,
      Their wings were blue,
      And they sang "Tilly-loo!"
    Till away they flew,--
And they never came back to me!
    They never came back!
    They never came back!
They never came back to me!

GREEN TIGER'S BOOK OF CHILDREN'S POETRY

Calico Jam,
    The little Fish swam,
Over the syllabub sea,
    He took off his hat,
    To the Sole and the Sprat,
    And the Willeby-Wat,--
But he never came back to me!
    He never came back!
    He never came back!
He never came back to me!

Calico Ban,
    The little Mice ran,
To be ready in time for tea,
    Flippity flup,
    They drank it all up,
    And danced in the cup,--
But they never came back to me!
    They never came back!
    They never came back!
They never came back to me!

GREEN TIGER'S BOOK OF CHILDREN'S POETRY

Calico Drum,
The Grasshoppers come,
The Butterfly, Beetle, and Bee,
Over the ground,
Around and around,
With a hop and a bound,--
But they never came back to me!
They never came back!
They never came back!
They never came back to me!

Edward Lear

THE RECIPE

'Round an' 'round, an' 'round we go
'Round the pan o' baking dough;
Pour molasses, sweet and thin,
Put a pinch o' ginger in,
Butter it an' roll it an'
Put it in another pan.
Bake it crisp and brown, and then,
Out jump twenty ginger men.

George Reiter Brill

OOM-PAH

OOM-PAH, boom-pah, oom-pah boom!
Like roses soon our cheeks will bloom.
We only ask for elbow-room
Oom-pah, boom-pah, oom-pah boom!

Hugh Lofting

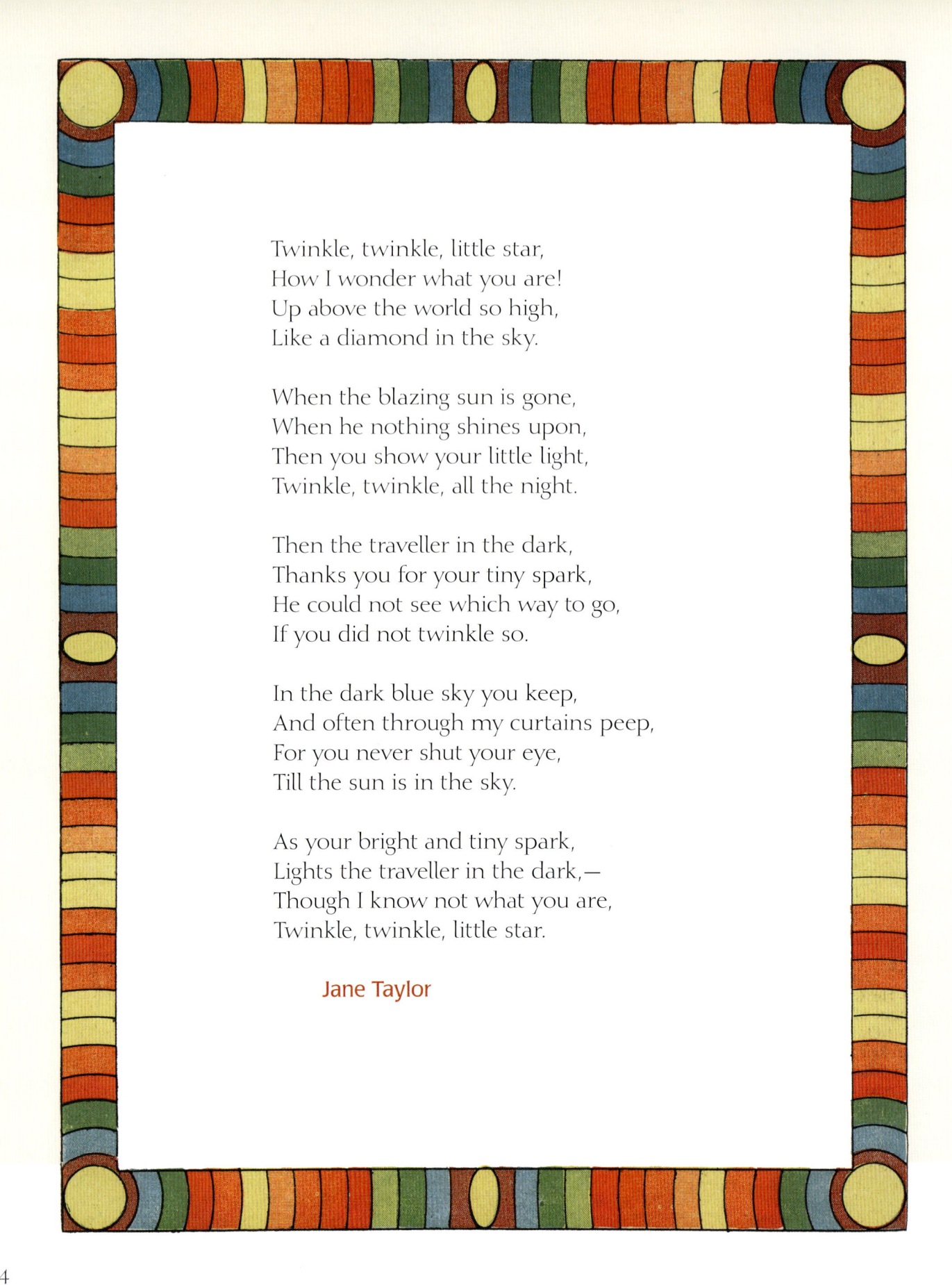

Twinkle, twinkle, little star,
How I wonder what you are!
Up above the world so high,
Like a diamond in the sky.

When the blazing sun is gone,
When he nothing shines upon,
Then you show your little light,
Twinkle, twinkle, all the night.

Then the traveller in the dark,
Thanks you for your tiny spark,
He could not see which way to go,
If you did not twinkle so.

In the dark blue sky you keep,
And often through my curtains peep,
For you never shut your eye,
Till the sun is in the sky.

As your bright and tiny spark,
Lights the traveller in the dark,—
Though I know not what you are,
Twinkle, twinkle, little star.

      Jane Taylor

GREEN TIGER'S BOOK OF CHILDREN'S POETRY

THE SHIP

I saw a ship a-sailing,
A-sailing on the sea;
And oh, it was all laden
With pretty things for thee!

There were comfits in the cabin,
And apples in the hold;
The sails were made of silk,
And the masts were made of gold.

The four-and-twenty sailors,
That stood between the decks,
Were four-and-twenty white mice,
With chains about their necks.

The captain was a duck,
With a jacket on his back;
And when the ship began to move,
The captain said, "Quack, Quack!"

Mother Goose

GREEN TIGER'S BOOK OF CHILDREN'S POETRY

FULL MOON

One night as Dick lay half asleep,
Into his drowsy eyes
A great still light began to creep
From out the silent skies.
It was the lovely moon's, for when
He raised his dreamy head,
Her surge of silver filled the pane
And streamed across his bed.
So, for a while, each gazed at each --
Dick and the solemn moon --
Till, climbing slowly on her way,
She vanished, and was gone.

    Walter de la Mare

GREEN TIGER'S BOOK OF CHILDREN'S POETRY

Blowing Bubbles! See how fine!
Look at Mine! O look at Mine!
How they dance, and how they shine—
Mine! Mine! Look at Mine!
Mine's like Water! Mine's like Wine!
Yours is not as big as Mine!

 Eleanor Farjeon

THE SUGAR-PLUM TREE

Have you ever heard of the Sugar-Plum Tree?
'Tis a marvel of great renown!
It blooms on the shore of the Lollipop sea
In the garden of Shut-Eye Town.
The fruit that it bears is so wondrously sweet
(As those who have tasted it say)
That good little children have only to eat
Of that fruit to be happy next day.

When you've got to the tree, you would have a hard time
To capture the fruit which I sing;
The tree is so tall that no person could climb
To the boughs where the sugar-plums swing!
But up in that tree sits a chocolate cat,
And a gingerbread dog prowls below--
And this is the way you contrive to get at
Those sugar-plums tempting you so:

You say but the word to that gingerbread dog
And he barks with such terrible zest
That the chocolate cat is at once all agog,
As her swelling proportions attest.
And the chocolate cat goes cavorting around
From this leafy limb unto that,
And the sugar-plums tumble, of course, to the ground--
Hurrah for that chocolate cat!

There are marshmallows, gumdrops, and peppermint canes,
With stripings of scarlet or gold,
And you carry away of the treasure that rains
As much as your apron can hold!
So come, little child, cuddle closer to me
In your dainty white nightcap and gown,
And I'll rock you away to that Sugar-Plum Tree
In the garden of Shut-Eye Town.

Eugene Field

CLOUD SHADOWS

I wish I could ride on the shadows of clouds
   That drift across the hill;
Over the meadows and out of sight
   They sweep so smooth and still.

Over the daisy-field they passed,
   And not a daisy stirred.
They moved like chariots grand and slow,
   But never a sound was heard.

I wish I could ride on the shadows of clouds
   Could ride till, the journey done,
I'd find myself at the end of the world,
   Where the earth and the sky are one.

Katharine Pyle

GREEN TIGER'S BOOK OF CHILDREN'S POETRY

My Feet they haul me Round the House
   They Hoist me up the Stairs;
I only have to Steer them, and
   They Ride me Everywheres!

Gelett Burgess

GREEN TIGER'S BOOK OF CHILDREN'S POETRY

JONATHAN BING DOES ARITHMETIC

When Jonathan Bing was young, they say,
He shirked his lessons and ran away,
Sat in a meadow and twiddled his thumbs
And never learnt spelling or did any sums.

So now if you tell him, "Add 1 to 2,"
"I don't understand!" he'll answer you;
"Do you mean 2-day or that's 2 bad?
And what sort of 1 do you want me to add?

For there's 1 who was first when the race was 1,
Though perhaps 2 many were trying to run,
So if 2 had 1 when the race was through,
I'd say the answer was 1 by 2!"

O Jonathan Bing, you haven't the trick
Of doing a sum in arithmetic!

Beatrice Curtis Brown

THE WIND

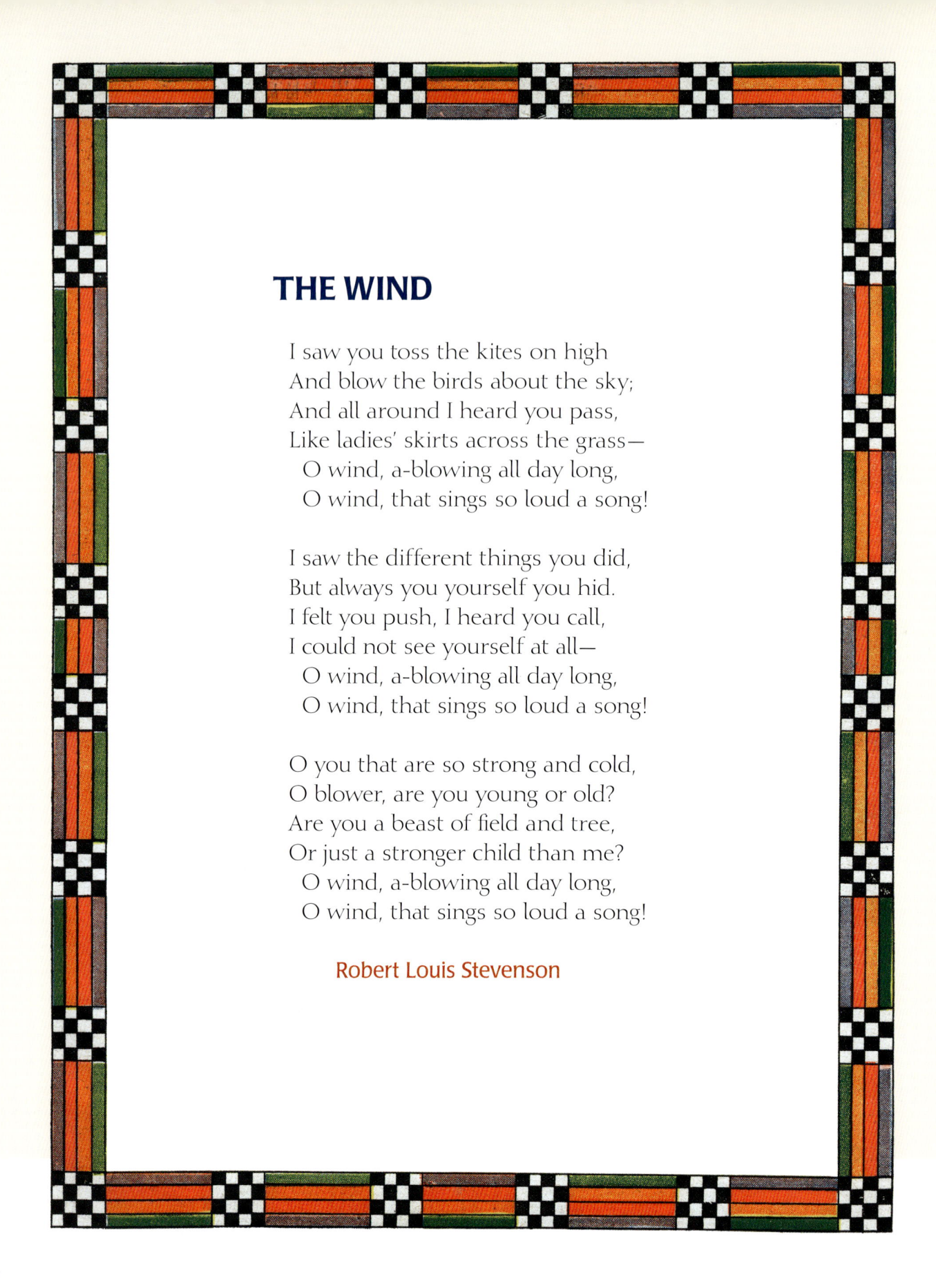

I saw you toss the kites on high
And blow the birds about the sky;
And all around I heard you pass,
Like ladies' skirts across the grass—
  O wind, a-blowing all day long,
  O wind, that sings so loud a song!

I saw the different things you did,
But always you yourself you hid.
I felt you push, I heard you call,
I could not see yourself at all—
  O wind, a-blowing all day long,
  O wind, that sings so loud a song!

O you that are so strong and cold,
O blower, are you young or old?
Are you a beast of field and tree,
Or just a stronger child than me?
  O wind, a-blowing all day long,
  O wind, that sings so loud a song!

Robert Louis Stevenson

GREEN TIGER'S BOOK OF CHILDREN'S POETRY

If ever you are feeling sad,
And find the world is gray!
You ought to try my splendid plan,
To send the dumps away.

Up to the nearest hill you run,
As hard as you can tear,
And then for fifteen times you take
A leap into the air.

And all the time you're leaping, you
A lullaby must sing;
And when you've done, you'll find you are
As pleased as anything.

Lewis Baumer

GREEN TIGER'S BOOK OF CHILDREN'S POETRY

THE FROG

Be kind and tender to the Frog,
And do not call him names,
As "Slimy skin," or "Polly-wog,"
Or likewise "Ugly James,"
Or "Gap-a-grin," or "Toad-gone-wrong,"
Or "Bill Bandy-knees":
The Frog is justly sensitive
To epithets like these.

No animal will more repay
A treatment kind and fair;
At least so lonely people say
Who keep a frog (and, by the way,
They are extremely rare).

Hilaire Belloc

GREEN TIGER'S BOOK OF CHILDREN'S POETRY

THE COW

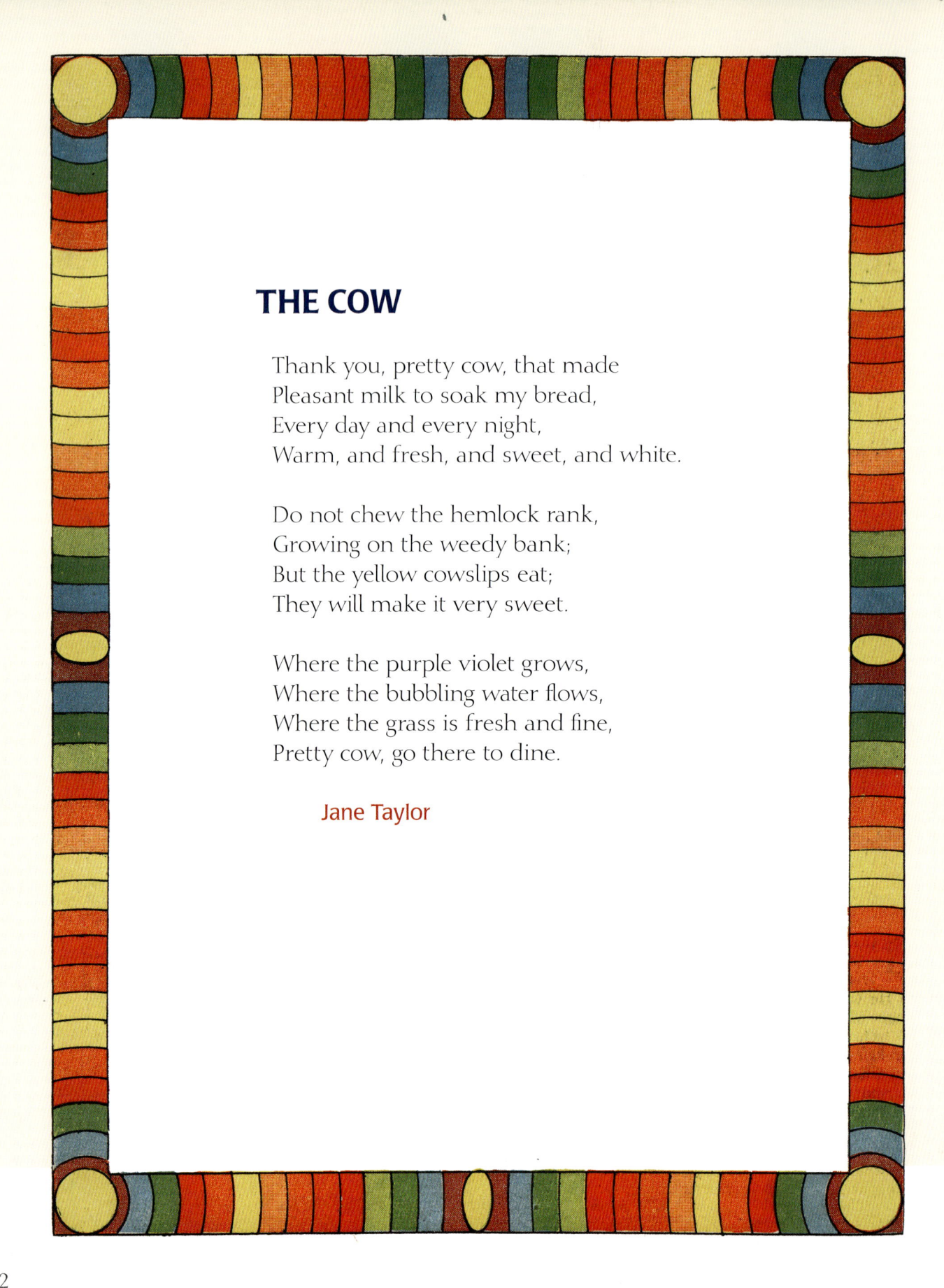

Thank you, pretty cow, that made
Pleasant milk to soak my bread,
Every day and every night,
Warm, and fresh, and sweet, and white.

Do not chew the hemlock rank,
Growing on the weedy bank;
But the yellow cowslips eat;
They will make it very sweet.

Where the purple violet grows,
Where the bubbling water flows,
Where the grass is fresh and fine,
Pretty cow, go there to dine.

  Jane Taylor

GREEN TIGER'S BOOK OF CHILDREN'S POETRY

103

CONTENTMENT

I like the way that the world is made,
(Tickle me, please, behind the ears)
With part in the sun and part in the shade
(Tickle me, please, behind the ears).
This comfortable spot beneath a tree
Was probably planned for you and me;
Why do you suppose God made a flea?
Tickle me more behind the ears.

I hear a cricket or some such bug
(Tickle me, please, behind the ears)
And there is a hole some creature dug
(Tickle me, please, behind the ears).
I can't quite smell it from where we sit,
But I think a rabbit would hardly fit;
Tomorrow, perhaps, I'll look into it:
Tickle me more behind the ears.

GREEN TIGER'S BOOK OF CHILDREN'S POETRY

A troublesome fly is near my nose,
(Tickle me, please, behind the ears);
He thinks I'll snap at him, I suppose,
(Tickle me, please, behind the ears).
If I lay on my back with my legs in air
Would you scratch my stomach, just here and there?
It's a puppy trick and I don't much care,
But tickle me more behind the ears.

Heaven, I guess, is all like this
(Tickle me, please, behind the ears);
It's my idea of eternal bliss
(Tickle me, please, behind the ears).
With angel cats for a dog to chase,
And a very extensive barking space,
And big bones buried all over the place, --
And you, to tickle behind my ears.

Burges Johnson

THE STARS

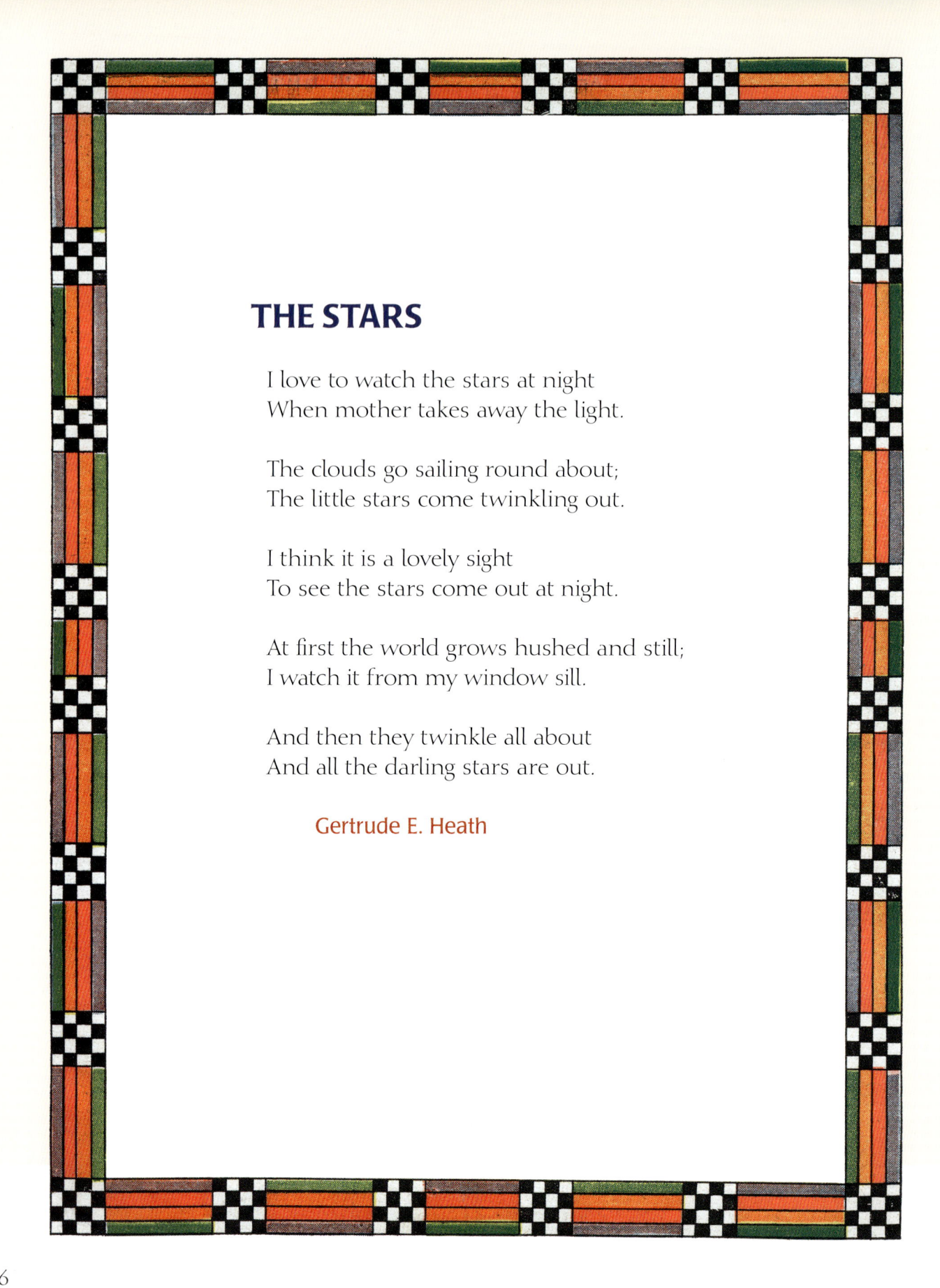

I love to watch the stars at night
When mother takes away the light.

The clouds go sailing round about;
The little stars come twinkling out.

I think it is a lovely sight
To see the stars come out at night.

At first the world grows hushed and still;
I watch it from my window sill.

And then they twinkle all about
And all the darling stars are out.

    Gertrude E. Heath

GREEN TIGER'S BOOK OF CHILDREN'S POETRY

THE ROCK-A-BY LADY

The Rock-a-by Lady from Hush-a-by Street
Comes stealing, comes creeping;
The poppies they hang from her head to her feet
And each hath a dream that is tiny and fleet,
She bringeth her poppies to you, my sweet,
When she findeth you sleeping!

There is one little dream of a beautiful drum,
"Rub-a-dub!" it goeth:
There is one little dream of a big sugar-plum,
And lo, thick and fast the other dreams come,
Of pop guns that bang, and tin tops that hum,
And a trumpet that bloweth!

And dollies peep out of those wee little dreams
With laughter and singing;
And boats go a-floating on silvery streams,
And the stars peek-a-boo with their own misty gleams,
And up, up and up, where the Mother Moon beams,
The fairies go winging!

Would you dream all these dreams that are tiny and fleet?
They'll come to you sleeping;
So shut the two eyes that are weary, my sweet,
For the Rock-a-by Lady from Hush-a by Street,
With poppies that hang from her head to her feet,
Comes stealing, comes creeping.

Eugene Field

GREEN TIGER'S BOOK OF CHILDREN'S POETRY

THE LAMPLIGHTER

My tea is nearly ready and the sun has left the sky;
It's time to take the window to see Leerie going by;
For every night at teatime and before you take your seat,
With lantern and with ladder he comes posting up the street.

Now Tom would be a driver and Maria go to sea,
And my papa's a banker and as rich as he can be;
But I, when I am stronger and can choose what I'm to do,
O Leerie, I'll go round at night and light the lamps with you!

For we are very lucky, with a lamp before the door,
And Leerie stops to light it as he lights so many more;
And oh! before you hurry by with ladder and with light;
O Leerie, see a little child and nod to him tonight!

Robert Louis Stevenson

GREEN TIGER'S BOOK OF CHILDREN'S POETRY

THE MILKY WAY

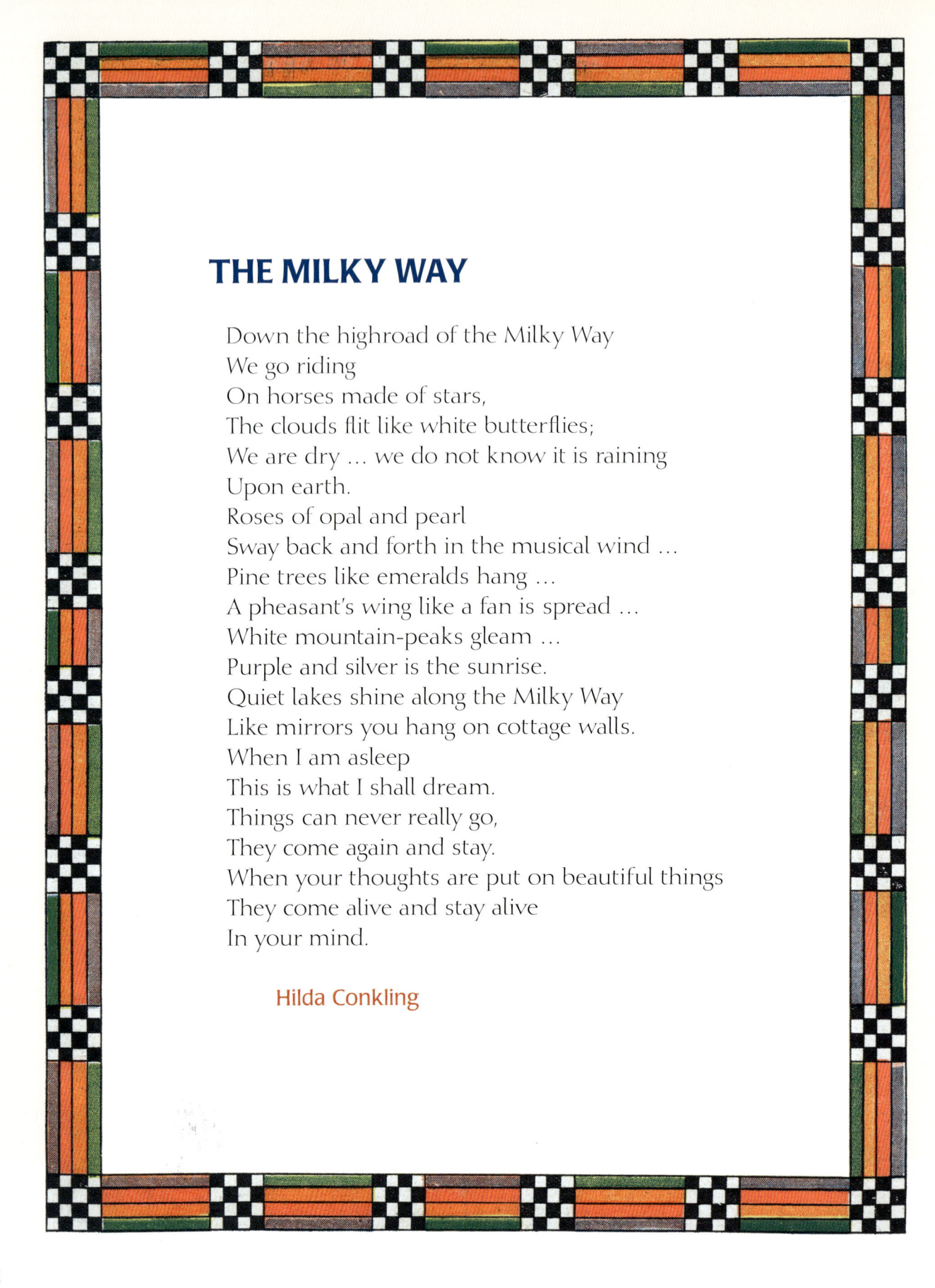

Down the highroad of the Milky Way
We go riding
On horses made of stars,
The clouds flit like white butterflies;
We are dry ... we do not know it is raining
Upon earth.
Roses of opal and pearl
Sway back and forth in the musical wind ...
Pine trees like emeralds hang ...
A pheasant's wing like a fan is spread ...
White mountain-peaks gleam ...
Purple and silver is the sunrise.
Quiet lakes shine along the Milky Way
Like mirrors you hang on cottage walls.
When I am asleep
This is what I shall dream.
Things can never really go,
They come again and stay.
When your thoughts are put on beautiful things
They come alive and stay alive
In your mind.

Hilda Conkling

GREEN TIGER'S BOOK OF CHILDREN'S POETRY

PIRATE STORY

Three of us afloat in the meadow by the swing,
   Three of us aboard in the basket on the lea.
Winds are in the air, they are blowing in the spring,
   And waves are on the meadow like the waves there are at sea.

Where shall we adventure, to-day that we're afloat,
   Wary of the weather and steering by a star?
Shall it be to Africa, a-steering of the boat,
   To Providence, or Babylon, or off to Malabar?

Hi! but here's a squadron a-rowing on the sea—
   Cattle on the meadow a-charging with a roar!
Quick, and we'll escape them, they're as mad as they can be,
   The wicket is the harbour and the garden is the shore.

   Robert Louis Stevenson

GREEN TIGER'S BOOK OF CHILDREN'S POETRY

Little Green Hummer

Little green Hummer
Was born in the summer;
His coat was as bright
As the emerald's light.
Short was his song,
Though his bill it was long;
His weight altogether
Not more than a feather.
From dipping his head
In the sunset red,
And gilding his side
In its fiery tide,
He gleamed like a jewel,
And darted around,

'Twixt sunlight and starlight,
Ne'er touching the ground.
Now over a blossom,
Now under, now in it;
Here, there, and everywhere,
All in a minute.
Ah! Never he cared
Who wondered and stared, —
His life was completeness
Of pleasure and sweetness;
He revelled in lightness,
In fleetness and brightness,
This sweet little Hummer
That came with the summer.

Mary Mapes Dodge

DUCKS' DITTY

All along the backwater
Through the rushes tall
Ducks are a-dabbling
Up tails all!

Ducks' tails, drakes' tails
Yellow feet a-quiver
Yellow bills all out of sight
Busy in the river!

Slushy green undergrowth
Where the roaches swim–
Here we keep our larder
Cold and cool and dim.

Everyone for what he likes!
We like to be
Heads down, tails up
Dabbling free!

High in the blue above
Swifts whirl and call–
We are down a-dabbling
Up tails all!

Kenneth Grahame

L'ENVOI

O seats of ancient learning; Philosophers and Sages,
A child has put a question, which I cannot find in pages
Of any book in any land; and so the answer's missed;
"Where do all the kisses go after they are kissed?"

Dorothy Una Ratcliffe

GREEN TIGER'S BOOK OF CHILDREN'S POETRY

I LAY MY BODY DOWN TO SLEEP
LET ANGELS GUARD MY HEAD
AND THROUGH THE HOURS OF
DARKNESS KEEP THEIR WATCH
AROUND MY BED

PICTURE CREDITS

Cover	Daniel Garber. "Orchard Window," n.d.
Endpapers	Frederick Richardson. From *Frederick Richardson's Book for Children*, 1938.
Half Title	Eulalie. From *The Bumper Book*, 1946.
Frontispiece	Jessie Willcox Smith. Magazine cover, c. 1930.
Title	Honor C. Appleton. From *The Bower Book of Simple Poems for Boys and Girls*, 1922.
2	Unknown. From *I Have a Little Shadow*, 1929.
5	N.C. Wyeth. From *Anthology of Children's Literature*, 1935.
7	Charles Folkard. From *Songs from Alice*, 1921.
8	Robert Lawson. From *Under the Tent of the Sky*, 1937.
9	Jessie Willcox Smith. From *A Child's Book of Old Verses*, 1935.
10	Marguerite Davis. From *Sing-Song*, 1924.
11	Charles Robinson. From *Nonsense Nonsense!* 1902.
12	Marchette Gaylord Chute. From *Rhymes About Ourselves*, 1932.
13	Harold Jones. From *Lavender's Blue*, 1954.
14 – 17	Willy Pogany. From *A Treasury of Verse for Little Children*, 1912.
18	Oliver Herford. From *The Kitten's Garden of Verses*, 1911.
19	Unknown. From *Isn't It Funny?* c. 1890.
21	H. Willebeek Le Mair. From *A Child's Garden of Verses*, 1926.
22	Adolf Zábransky. From *Ring-a-Ling*, c. 1960.
23	Flora Smith. From *My Poetry Book*, 1954.
24 – 27	L. Leslie Brooke. From *Nonsense Songs*, c. 1900.
28 – 29	A. Nobody. From *A Nobody's Nonsense*, c. 1898.
30	Clara M. Burd. *From A Child's Garden of Verses*, 1929.
31	M. Dibdin Spooner. From *The Golden Staircase*, 1910.
33 – 34	Gertrude A. Kay. From *Some Poems of Childhood*, 1931.
35	Willard Bonte. From *A Bedtime Book of Sandman Rhymes*, 1904.
37	John Hassall. From *Six and Twenty Boys and Girls*, c. 1902.
38	J.G. Francis. From *A Book of Cheerful Cats and Other Animated Animals*, 1879.
39	Eulalie. From *The Bumper Book*, 1946.
40 – 41	Edward Lear. From *A Book of Nonsense*, c. 1885.
43	Honor C. Appleton. From *The Bower Book of Simple Poems for Boys and Girls*, 1922.
44	Hugh Lofting. From *Porridge Poetry*, 1924.
45	Phyllis Britcher. From *The Rhyme and Picture Book*, 1936.
46 – 47	Jessie Willcox Smith. From *A Child's Garden of Verses*, 1905.
48	Vachel Lindsay. From *Every Soul is a Circus*, 1929.

PICTURE CREDITS

49	Adolf Zábransky.	From *Ring-a-Ling*, c. 1960.
51	H. Willebeek Le Mair.	From *A Child's Garden of Verses*, 1926.
52	Marguerite David.	From *Tirra Lirra: Rhymes Old and New*, 1955.
53	Frances Tipton Hunter.	From *The Frances Tipton Hunter Picture Book*, 1935.
55	Margaret W. Tarrant.	From *Verses for Children*, 1918.
57	Willy Pogany.	From *A Treasury of Verse for Little Children*, 1923.
58	B.T.B. and Nicolas Bentley.	From *Hilaire Belloc's Cautionary Verses*, 1931.
59	Gelett Burgess.	From *The Purple Cow*, 1894.
61	Jessie Willcox Smith.	From *A Child's Book of Old Verses*, 1935.
62	Peter Newell.	From *The Merry-Go-Round*, 1901.
63	Blanche Fisher Wright.	From *The Peter Patter Book*, 1918.
65	Willy Pogany.	From *A Treasury of Verse for Little Children*, 1912.
67	William Nicholson.	From *The Square Book of Animals*, 1900.
68	Robert Lawson.	From *Under the Tent of the Sky*, 1937.
69	Margaret Tarrant.	From *Rhymes of Old Times*, 1925.
71	Cecily Mary Barker.	From *A Little Book of Rhymes New and Old*, c. 1937.
73	Charles Robinson.	From *Nonsense Nonsense!* 1902.
74	Helen Sewell.	From *The Dream Keeper and Other Poems*, 1932.
75	Millicent Sowerby.	From *A Child's Garden of Verses*, 1908.
76 - 77	Jessie Willcox Smith.	From *A Child's Book of Old Verses*, 1935.
78 – 81	L. Leslie Brooke.	From *Nonsense Songs*, c. 1900.
82	George Reiter Brill.	From *Rhymes of the Golden Age*, 1908.
83	Hugh Lofting.	From *Porridge Poetry*, 1924.
85	Jessie Willcox Smith.	From *A Child's Book of Old Verses*, 1935.
86 - 87	Alan Wright.	From *My Picture Story Book*, 1925.
88	W. Heath Robinson.	From *Peacock Pie*, 1924.
89	Cecily Mary Barker.	From *A Little Book of Rhymes New and Old*, c. 1937.
91	Anne Anderson.	From *The Sleepy-Song Book*, c. 1920.
93	Sarah S. Stilwell.	From *Childhood*, 1904.
94	Gelett Burgess.	From *The Burgess Nonsense Book*, 1901.
95	Robert Lawson.	From *Just For Fun*, 1940.
96 – 97	Florence Edith Storer.	From *A Child's Garden of Verses*, 1909.
98 – 99	Lewis Baumer.	From *Did You Ever?* 1910
100 – 101	B.T.B. and Nicolas Bentley.	From *Hilaire Belloc's Cautionary Verses*, 1931.
102 – 103	Alan Wright.	From *My Picture Story Book*, 1925.
104 – 105	Edwina.	From *Sonnets from the Pekinese*, 1936.
107	Jan Cragin.	From *Sing, Little Birdie*, 1928.

PICTURE CREDITS

        109   Willy Pogany. From *My Poetry Book*, 1948.
   110 – 111   Lois Lenski. From *Fireside Poems*, 1930.
        113   Dorothy P. Lathrop. From *Silverhorn: The Hilda Conkling Book for Other Children*, 1924.
   114 – 115   Florence Edith Storer. From *A Child's Garden of Verses*, 1909.
        116   Sarah S. Stilwell. From *Rhymes and Jingles*, 1904.
        117   Masha. From *The Golden Almanac*, 1944.
        118   Cecile Walton. From *Nightlights*, 1929.
        119   Mrs. Arthur Gaskin. From *Divine and Moral Songs for Children*, 1896.
        123   Adolf Zábransky. From *Ring-a-Ling*, c. 1960.
Back Cover   Unknown. Advertisement, n.d.

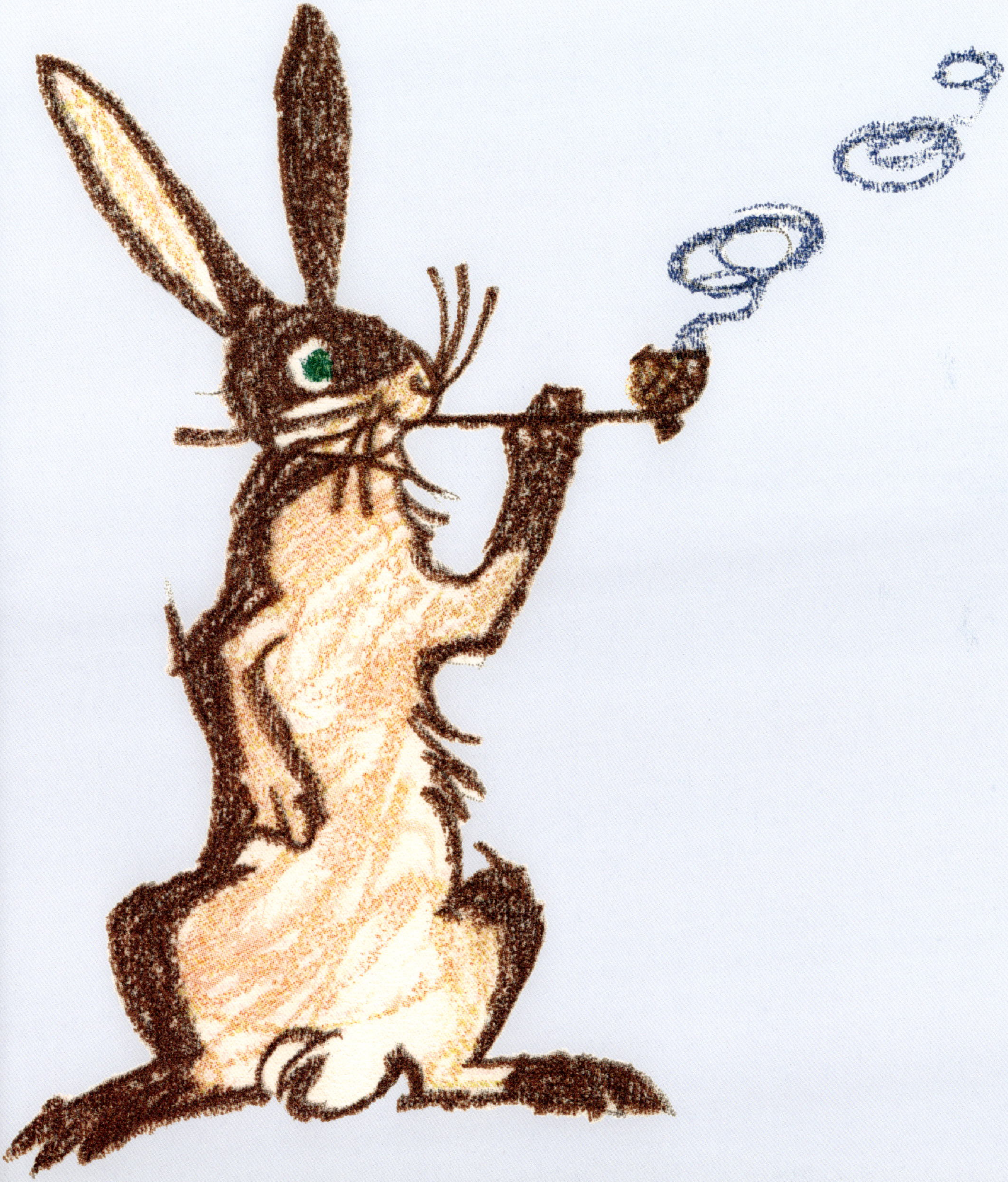